Love Untamed

Romances of the Old West

JoAnn Chartier
Chris Enss

TWODOT®

Guilford, Connecticut

An imprint of The Globe Pequot Press

A · TWODOT® · BOOK

TwoDot is a registered trademark of The Globe Pequot Press.

Illustrations by JoAnn Chartier
Text design by Lisa Reneson

Library of Congress Cataloging-in-Publication Data.

Chartier, JoAnn.
    Love untamed : romances of the Old West / JoAnn Chartier and Chris Enss.
        p. cm.
    Includes bibliographical references and index.
    ISBN 0-7627-1142-6
    1. Man-woman relationships. 2. Love. 3. Frontier and pioneer life—West (U.S.) 4. Pioneers—United States—History. I. Title: romances of the Old West. II. Enss, Chris, 1961– III. Title.

HQ801.A2 C48 2002
306.7—dc21

                                                                2002021512

Manufactured in the United States of America
First Edition/Fourth Printing

To John: For making so many things possible
—Chris Enss

To my grandchildren: Love made you; love keeps you
—JoAnn Chartier

Acknowledgments

The authors wish to express appreciation for the able assistance of a number of research librarians, historians, and individuals who tracked down material for this book. In libraries as far-flung as Alaska and Texas, assistance was provided in searching out original sources, historical newspapers and periodicals, photographs, and anecdotal material. The collection of interviews with acquaintances of Margaret and Marcus Daly published by Ada Powell, as well as her personal notes, provided insight into the characters of two controversial people whose personal and business papers were deliberately destroyed.

The introduction and inventory of papers and photographs of Frances Noyes Muncaster prepared by Louetta Ward were invaluable. The "Handbook of Texas Online," a joint project of the General Libraries of Texas at Austin and the Texas State Historical Society, is a researcher's dream come true. Thanks to Dean Rudy for his Web site "Mountain Men and the Fur Trade."

The authors also wish to express gratitude to the staffs of the following societies, university libraries, and organizations for their help in gathering information and photographs for this book: Alaska State Library; Fayetteville Historical Society, Fayetteville, Arkansas; Garst Museum & The Darke County Historical Society, Greenville, Ohio; Nevada County Historical Society, Nevada City, California; Panhandle Plains Historical Museum; University of Montana, Missoula, Archives; Utah Historical Society; Washington State Historical Society; Wyoming State Archives Department, Cody, Wyoming; and Yukon Archives, University of Alaska Fairbanks.

Special thanks to Charlene Patterson for her brilliant editing skills and for carefully guiding this book through the publishing process, and to Chris's sister-in-law, Monica Parry, for her keen eye and gentle critique.

Contents

Introduction

Probably no other topic in the history of writing has generated as many words as the subject of love. Songs, poems, books, plays, operas, and films have celebrated the joys and bemoaned the woes of love. In this book the theme is narrowed to thirteen true stories of love in the early days of the westward expansion of America.

The territory covered here ranges from Alaska's goldfields to the Texas Panhandle, and the time period starts in the early 1830s, in the days of the fur trappers, and progresses to the Wild West shows that celebrated the adventures of the frontier in the early part of the twentieth century. The love affairs of these thirteen couples represent the variety of relationships that added color, controversy, and commitment to the unmatched days of the Old West.

In these pages you'll find ladies of the night whose hearts longed for true love and spinsters who wanted to love God rather than any man. There are outlaws, both male and female, who yearned for what they knew they couldn't have, and there are couples who had it all and nearly lost it.

The times and settings in which these romances took place greatly influenced them. There was undoubtedly more freedom from the social conventions of the "civilized" East, but old customs and beliefs still carried an influence in the West. Actresses were considered by upper-crust society to be barely a step above prostitutes. Proper ladies of the East were not allowed to be alone in the same room with an unmarried man, whereas a western saloon girl was expected to be "friendly" with the customers.

The bumpy road to romance was just as rocky in the "good old days" as it is now. Not every story here has a happy ending, but all these tales reflect the lives and times—and loves—of the people who settled the West.

La Bonté haunted by the memory of Mary Brand

The Trapper and the Girl He Left Behind

LA BONTÉ AND MARY BRAND

You cannot pay a trapper a greater compliment, than to persuade him you have mistaken him for an Indian brave; and, in truth, the counterfeit is complete.

—WASHINGTON IRVING, *The Adventures of Captain Bonneville, 1849*

Wisps of smoke drifted upward from a small campfire. A sky like black velvet, scattered with icy white diamond chips, arched overhead, its edges scalloped by the ragged black lace of tall trees. From somewhere behind the trapper limned in the firelight came the disembodied call of an owl, "Who . . . who . . . oo whoooo."

La Bonté shivered slightly. He knew very well who was haunting him. Mary. As if her name were an incantation, the smoke writhed gently, twining and curving to show him her beloved form, the beautiful face and graceful neck, the thick, dark-brown hair heavy on her little head.

As if it were yesterday, he recalled the last time he'd seen her, had felt her hands clinging desperately to his. Her eyes were bathed in tears; her pink mouth trembled in a brave effort to stem the tide of anguish. She'd vowed her love despite the stain of blood on his hands.

The smoke eddied; the image dissolved. He'd not seen Mary in nearly fifteen long years. The bullet that had gouged a path across his neck hadn't hurt him as much as his heart the day he'd left her behind in Tennessee. Absently, he rubbed at the scar. He had more scars than he could count now. And he'd killed more men. Indians they were, who fought amongst themselves and against any white strangers who came into their territory seeking the wealth of beaver pelts and buffalo hides to be had in the Rocky Mountains.

La Bonté moved restlessly. The last thing he'd wanted to do was kill his friend, Pete. Jealousy had been at the root of it—jealousy and the wild blood of young men. He didn't blame Mary, for he'd known even then that her love for him was true. She'd be married now, he told himself, married and surrounded by strapping sons and lovely daughters. It was a lucky man who'd won Mary's heart. With the heel of his hand, La Bonté rubbed the ache in his chest through the fringed buckskins he wore. Then he rose to his feet and walked away from the campfire to check his animals. Dwelling on the past could get a man killed, he thought to himself, for he'd lost the keen edge of awareness when he'd abandoned himself to dreams of the past.

La Bonté was uncommonly good looking. He was tall and had dark hair and clean-shaven cheeks. His father was French, from St. Louis, his mother a native of Tennessee. Only twenty years old when he turned away from all he loved to head west, La Bonté had quickly learned how to survive in a beautiful, but often deadly, land.

By 1847 he and a companion named Killbuck were in what is now South Pass, Colorado, at a place near Boiling Spring. Little did he know that across the prairie to the east a wagon train jolted slowly toward South Pass, carrying Mary Brand and her family closer to the Rockies.

Mary's father knew the dangers he and his family faced. He also knew there was strength in numbers, so he'd decided to travel with a band of Mormons headed for Utah. His two grown sons were strong and stouthearted, their wives and children sturdy and willing. His daughter Mary had weathered the heartbreak of her youth and was good-tempered and industrious as well as remarkably beautiful. But she'd never married. People said that her heart had been broken, and no man had ever been able to rekindle the flame in her breast, though many had tried. Mary knew she would never wed. She'd had her chance and had thrown it away over a bit of girlish foolishness.

Only once in fifteen years had Mary heard of the one she'd loved. Two years after her lover had fled to the West, a mountain man from the frontier had returned to Tennessee. Hearing him recounting tales of a trapper's life, she haltingly asked after the man who'd left her behind.

The weathered face of the old mountaineer had lit up. Of course, he knew La Bonté well. Alas, he'd heard at one of the forts that the famous mountaineer had been "killed on the Yellow Stone by Blackfeet."

Devastated to have her worst fears given voice, Mary hid her heartbreak and never spoke again of the young man she'd hoped to marry. She stayed devoted to her family and her brother's children. She knew she would have no children of her own.

When her father decided to set out for California, Mary could not help but think of La Bonté, lost to her for so long. A flicker of hope leapt inside her, and dreams of miraculous meetings tormented her sleep. Wouldn't she have felt it if the heart of her true love had stopped beating? Wouldn't the sunshine have dimmed, the birds have mourned, when he breathed his last? In one secret corner of her heart lived a flickering hope that perhaps the old trapper had been wrong.

La Bonté had no hope at all. His memories deviled him in the cool of the evening when he sat alone beside a campfire, listening to the night. In the first years of his flight, he'd lost sleep over the

images crowding his fevered brain: Mary's willowy form, her brilliant eyes and sweet smile; and Big Pete, his friend until that fateful
day at a corn husking when suddenly he became a rival. The two
had hunted together as boys, until jealousy over Mary came between
them. Even now, fifteen years later, La Bonté could feel the boiling
heat of rage at the memory of Pete triumphantly snatching a kiss
from Mary.

Everyone at the corn shucking party had seen it. Scarcely aware
of what he was doing, La Bonté had seized a small keg of whiskey
and hurled it at Pete. The room went still, and La Bonté challenged
Pete to "follow if he was a man."

Outside, friends of the two young men arranged a duel. Mary
collapsed in grief and terror. Her father locked her and the other
women in the house. All the men gathered at the field, where the
two rivals stood braced at forty paces, their rifle butts on the
ground, their hunting pouches full of ammunition hanging over
their shoulders.

La Bonté and Pete were each about 6 feet tall, young and
strong, and both knew the frontier rules of dueling. Once the signal
was given, they would fire until one or the other dropped. The order
to fire was called out; the men raised their rifles and fired. Both
were seen to jerk slightly, as if a bullet had struck, but they held
their positions.

The crowd pressed forward as the two men began to reload
their rifles. Blood ran freely down La Bonté's neck from a gash on
the left side; Pete pressed a hand momentarily to his chest as if
checking the position of a wound. Then, in the act of forcing the
next bullet down the barrel of his rifle with a hickory stick, Pete let
the weapon slip from his hand. His arm dropped; he swayed like a
tree in a strong wind and fell to the ground, dead.

In the house Mary froze at the sound of shots; she strained to hear. Pounding against the locked door she cried out for release, for help, for someone to tell her if her lover had died. Minutes ticked by like hours. No one came to bring her news. By the time she learned what had happened, La Bonté had escaped to the woods, wary of the law.

Mary was filled with remorse for teasing Big Pete and intentionally stirring the flame of jealousy in La Bonté. It had been only a momentary impulse to test La Bonté's devotion. She'd not thought it could lead to this. Big Pete was dead, killed by the friend of his youth, and La Bonté must leave the community, leaving her behind, possibly forever.

For La Bonté, the first days of living off the land in the woods of Tennessee had fixed his fate. He'd always been fascinated by fur trappers and explorers and the tales they told of an almost untracked land to the west. Something in the wind from the frontier called to him, had always called, and now he had no choice but to heed the summons.

Before he left he slipped back to the village and into Mary's arms for one last kiss. Then he set out for the West, traveling from the Yellowstone country to the Wind River Range and all the way to California and New Mexico, but always returning to the Rockies. He trapped beaver and chased buffalo, fought some Indians and traded with others. He dressed in fringed buckskins and moccasins made by Indian women. His hair was shoulder length, his barber the keen edge of his own blade. He slept in a shaggy buffalo skin beside a campfire, with one eye peeled and one ear cocked for danger.

He hadn't made his fortune. And fifteen years in the rough company of mountain men and Indians, battling the elements and wandering from one camp to another, had rubbed away any manners his mother had taught him. Still, he was considered a prize catch by many Indian maidens. But he could not forget a certain blue-eyed girl in Tennessee, and though he really harbored no hope of seeing her again, he'd saved one soft beaver pelt for the woman who haunted his lonely nights.

It was now 1847 and, unbeknownst to La Bonté, the object of his memories was drawing closer as the Brand family slowly traveled across the plains. Mary's dreams were fired anew by tales told around the campfire by Antoine, the Canadian guide hired by her father. Antoine frequently mentioned a legendary hunter named La Bonté, but it was a common enough name, and at first Mary felt only the faintest spark from that flickering memory hidden deep in a corner of her heart.

Finally, almost afraid to ask, she spoke the question, "Who was this La Bonté, Antoine, who you say was so brave a mountaineer?"

"He is a handsome man, strong and brave, unafraid of the savages," Antoine explained. "He rides like a Comanche, shoots true; he traps beaver and sells their pelts for plenty of money, but he's openhanded with his friends; he hunts with Blackfoot and Cheyenne all around the mountains."

Could this man be her love? Mary's heart was wrenched to hear that this mountain man had plenty of money, yet he did not return to his home. But it probably was not the man she loved. Surely he would have returned to her if he could. She settled back, convinced it was only a man with the same name.

But Antoine, in the way of a storyteller, was not finished with the tale. The guide told her that La Bonté loved the mountains more than he loved the grand houses of St. Louis or Montreal. And, he added sadly, the girl he'd fought a duel for did not love him, so he'd vowed never to return to his home.

Mary gasped in shock. Antoine continued, saying that La Bonté had gone all the way to California, where perhaps he'd been killed and scalped.

Mary's heart was breaking. "Are you sure?" she cried.

Antoine, seeing the distress in her trembling hands and white cheeks, guessed the truth. "Maybe he's not gone. It's hard to kill a mountain man," he confided. Trappers may go down ten times, but likely as not they'll turn up twenty times, he assured her.

Mary scarcely knew what to believe. Despite Antoine's attempts to relieve her dismay, she burst into tears. Hope and fear waged a battle inside her heart. All the love she had once felt returned in a violent grief that she might have lost her beloved a second time.

Heavy of heart, Mary scarcely noticed when her father's three wagons split away from the party of Mormons and set out alone toward South Pass. Antoine, scouting ahead, sighted a war party on an upland ridge and warned everyone of the danger. Each night the Brand party drew the wagons tightly together, and each day the men rode with their rifles ready.

They warned the women and children to stay close even in daylight. Slowly they made their way closer to South Pass, while miles away La Bonté and Killbuck were swapping tales with a British stranger they'd just met named George Frederick Ruxton. Ruxton idly related the news of the Mormon party and the foolish family that had separated and started alone for the Platte and South Pass. Old Killbuck shook his head at their folly, "They'll lose their hair, I'm thinking, if the Rapahos are out."

"I hope not," Ruxton said, "for there's a young woman amongst them worth more than that."

La Bonté sat cleaning his rifle. He looked up with some sympathy, saying he hated to think of a white woman in the hands of Indians. "Where does she come from?" he asked.

When he learned the family was from Tennessee, a flood of memories flowed through him, but before he could learn more,

Killbuck's mule pricked its ears and sampled the air. La Bonté rose abruptly, knowing the mule scented Indians.

Poised with rifles ready, the three men waited as a lone Indian walked into their camp, gesturing and explaining in Spanish and English that he was hungry. Killbuck and La Bonté conversed with the man, fed him as much as he could hold, and provided powder for his gun. In return he revealed the latest news: A war party was headed for the divide, and they intended to wipe out everything in white skin they came across. Three wagons were known to be traveling alone toward the pass.

The British hunter frowned, recalling the beautiful young woman. "Those are the wagons belonging to old Brand," he announced, "and he's started alone for Laramie."

"Brand!" La Bonté had never forgotten the name. Fear coalesced in his heart. He could not ignore danger to members of that family. Telling his comrades he intended to warn the party, he urged his horse to a hard trot down the trail. Killbuck and the other hunter followed.

But they were at least a day away.

Deducing that the Indians he had spotted were out to kill whites and steal horses, Antoine issued rapid orders. The women and children were secured inside the wagons; the men were all armed and told to keep a sharp eye on everything that moved. At Black Horse Creek they set up camp, pulling the wagons together to provide as much protection as possible. But the horses needed to be watered and fed, so Brand's sons and grandsons took the animals a short distance to water and good grass after warning the women and children not to wander.

After they had gone, several Indians appeared in the Brands' camp. Only Mary's father and a fourteen-year-old grandson were in the camp with Mary and the other women. They nervously watched as the Indians, making signs of peace, approached. Uneasy, Brand was cautiously hospitable, until the Indians began picking up items around the camp as if expecting a gift.

Brand shook his head, holding his temper until the Indians began to walk away with some of the items, including a pot of boiling water. Brand yanked it away and knocked the thief down. One of the other Indians jerked the buckskin cover from his gun, ready to avenge his companion. Mary dashed up and put her hands on the gun cover and a pistol against the Indian's chest.

This act of bravery seemed to impress the Indian, who motioned to the others to keep the peace. When the other members of the Brand family returned to camp, they all sat down and ate supper together, after which the Indians departed. Antoine, expecting the worst, set up a guard, but the night passed without incident.

La Bonté, Killbuck, and Ruxton encountered the signs of wagons that day, but they had to camp for the night before they could catch up with the travelers. La Bonté was restless and haunted as the stars wheeled across the sky. He wondered if the wagons they were trailing actually belonged to the family of Mary Brand. He vowed to himself that he would lend whatever aid he could and waited for the first glimmer of dawn, anxious to catch up with the small party.

After a tense night listening to prairie wolves howl, the Brand party was up before sunrise. As they were yoking the oxen to the wagons, a band of Indians appeared against the pale sky. They loped their ponies down the bluff, and Antoine immediately noticed their war paint and weapons.

They demanded powder and lead, and when they were refused, they warned that "their eyes were red with blood so they could not tell the difference between white and Yutah scalps."

Brand saw that all the wagons were hitched and the drivers

poised, whips in hand. With a curse he turned and gave the signal to start, then moved toward his horse. Just as he leapt for the saddle, an Indian jumped him and pulled him down. The Indian drew back his bow, ready to shoot, but fell before the arrow could fly; Brand had pulled out a pistol and fired straight into the Indian's chest. Then Brand went down under the war club of another attacker.

When Mary saw her father struck down, she sprang forward with a cry. An Indian brandished a knife over the old man's prostrate form, ready to take his hair. Screaming, she dashed toward her father. Suddenly she was jerked down, a noose, thrown by one of the raiding party, tight around her body. An arrow flew in her direction; she struggled wildly to her knees but was yanked down again. With a wild yell the Indian dropped the rope and pulled his knife as he rushed toward the helpless quarry.

At that moment a bellow of rage whipped everyone around toward its source. La Bonté plunged down the steep slope toward the battle, his rifle in hand, long hair and buckskin fringes whipped by the wind. Catching sight of the young woman in the hands of the Indian, he spurred his horse straight across the battleground.

Eyes closed against the murderous weapon she expected to descend at any moment, Mary heard the fierce battle cry and opened her eyes in time to see a wild mountaineer strike a mighty blow that carried her attacker away. Struggling against the lasso that still bound her arms, she watched as three white men charged into the fray. The Indians, apparently believing an advance guard of a larger force was attacking, quickly fled in the opposite direction.

La Bonté turned his horse as the attackers fled, returning to the woman tangled in the long buckskin rope. Jumping from his horse, he slashed the bonds and raised her from the ground. She looked up into his eyes and the thanks died on her lips as she beheld the face of her beloved. Trembling, scarcely able to believe, she stared as his rugged countenance paled.

"What, Mary! Can it be you?" he cried hoarsely.

"You don't forget me!"she sobbed, falling into his arms.

The Brand family pulled itself together, exclaiming over the miracle that had led La Bonté and his friends to them in their hour of greatest need. The three mountain men accompanied the wagons on the rest of their journey, and no other attacks occurred. Mary rode a mustang by La Bonté's side, unwilling to spend another moment apart from him.

Still, she caught him staring deep into the mountains, longing, she feared, for the freedom and adventure of a trapper's life. She struggled against her fears that her love was not enough to hold him, until at last La Bonté revealed his heart; it was hard to leave old friends behind, but Mary, he said, was forever his love.

They were married at the first opportunity and had children of their own who were blessed with a love of mountains from their father and the steadfast heart of their mother.

Isabella Bird

The Outlaw and the Parson's Daughter

JIM NUGENT AND ISABELLA BIRD

His heart is good and kind, as good a heart as ever beat. He's a great enemy of his own.
—RANCHER GRIFF EVANS'S DESCRIPTION OF ROCKY MOUNTAIN JIM

I sabella Bird drew in a deep breath of air so pure it made her giddy. Her heart beat faster. The long climb high into Colorado's Rocky Mountains was almost at an end. The trail before her opened into a narrow valley. A small, dark building with smoke eddying from the roof gave promise that the man she'd come so far to find was at home. She'd been warned against this journey, warned against seeking out this outlaw. Most people thought it was scandalous that the daughter of a clergyman was seeking a meeting with a notorious outlaw. Rocky Mountain Jim was a desperado, a ruffian, a legend in the West, and not suitable for an English lady's company.

Isabella smiled to herself; the legend was almost within reach. She glanced at her unhappy escort. The young man and a friend had reluctantly agreed to guide her to Estes Park from Longmount, Colorado. The two men were newly graduated law students, out for one last hunting trip before beginning their careers in a law office, but the friend had taken off to hunt on his own. The young guide at

Isabella's side seemed less than enthusiastic now that the outlaw's den lay before them.

She urged her rented horse forward, eager to meet the object of her 1,000-mile odyssey that had begun in sophisticated San Francisco and promised success in the rugged Colorado Rockies.

Down in Muggins Gulch, inside the primitive cabin, a man sat staring at the fire. He no longer noticed the litter of rough living in his shabby log house. The wisps of hay, old blankets, tanned skins, and moccasins strewn about with horseshoes, magazines, bones, tin cans, firewood, and stacks of books didn't bother him. The things he needed most, such as the powder flasks and two very fine rifles, were in excellent condition and easily accessible, and the whiskey bottle was full.

His dog, Ring, jumped up from the hearth, barking an alarm as he rushed out the door. The man frowned at the thought of visitors. He liked his privacy and guarded it well. Irritated, he rose and stared outside, instantly measuring and dismissing the young man on the horse. Then he set eyes on the other rider, a woman, an astonishing woman riding through the narrow defile leading into Muggins Gulch, into the very dooryard of the outlaw guarding the entrance to Estes Park.

Jim Nugent stepped outside to greet this unexpected visitor. The curse that rose so easily to his lips was stifled at the last second.

Isabella Bird shaded her eyes. She saw a figure emerge from the dark cabin and kick at the dog. The young man at her side muttered something unintelligible and checked his gun. Isabella sat straighter in the saddle as her horse drew closer. She tried not to stare.

The one-eyed ruffian barred the trail. Dressed in ragged layers, with a pistol in the breast pocket of his coat and a knife in his belt, the outlaw known as Rocky Mountain Jim gazed at her with one piercing blue eye. Isabella wondered if she'd made a mistake.

Rocky Mountain Jim Nugent

"Desperado was written in large letters all over him. I almost repented of having sought his acquaintance," she later wrote her sister, Henrietta.

Isabella studied the man she'd heard so much about. She wrote that he was

> a broad, thickset man, about middle height, with an old cap
> on his head, and wearing a grey hunting suit much the worse
> for wear (almost falling to pieces in fact) a digger's scarf

15

knotted round his waist, a knife in his belt, and a "bosom friend," a revolver, sticking out of the breast pocket of his coat; his feet, which were very small, were bare, except for some dilapidated moccasins made of horsehide. The marvel was how his clothes hung together, and on him.

It had been a very long time since Jim Nugent had heard the cultured tones of an Englishwoman. Not since his youth had he had reason to call on the manners drummed into him by his doting mother. Conscious of his frightful appearance yet eager to converse with this unexpected visitor, he mustered his best behavior and offered her water, apologizing that he had nothing better than a battered tin can from which to drink.

"We entered into conversation, and as he spoke I forgot both his reputation and appearance, for his manner was that of a chivalrous gentleman, his accent refined, and his language easy and elegant," wrote Isabella. But his face could not be ignored for long. "One eye was entirely gone, and the loss made one side of his face repulsive, while the other might have been modeled in marble." His one eye, she wrote, "was large, gray-blue and deeply set beneath well-marked eyebrows." His nose she described as "aquiline", his mouth "very handsome." He was "smooth shaven except for a dense mustache and imperial," or short, pointed beard in fashion at the time.

Like Isabella, Mountain Jim had come to terms with the difficulties of life. But where she had taken the high road, he had steadily followed the low, until that September day when the parson's petite, intelligent, and cultivated daughter rode down the trail to his cabin.

He couldn't help but wonder if she knew his name was used to frighten children into good behavior. Had she heard of his early exploits as a scout? Surely, he thought, she would not have conversed with him so willingly if she knew of his reputation as a member of an outlaw band.

She did know, but she still asked Rocky Mountain Jim to be her guide, despite the fact that her neighbors back in Yorkshire would have been horrified. Her father was an Anglican clergyman, her mother's family included a bishop. She had one sister, Henrietta, a timid soul content to stay in the small village of their youth. Isabella, on the other hand, seemed to come to life as soon as she left behind the confines and strictures placed on a clergyman's daughter. Despite chronic pain from a childhood condition and the difficulties faced by a single woman traveling alone, Isabella thrived in unfamiliar territory and in primitive conditions.

Isabella's ill health as a child had caused her parents great concern. Surgery to remove a spinal tumor when she was eighteen had left her in great pain, unable to raise her head for weeks. Finally, hoping that a change of scenery would help, her father took the family to the Scottish Highlands for the summer. Isabella revived in the new environment and with the relative freedom from the social conventions of Yorkshire. Her health again declined when the family returned home. That pattern continued. While traveling, Isabella's health improved; back home, it failed. Finally in 1854, when she was twenty-three, her father handed her one hundred pounds and told her to travel where she liked for as long as the money lasted.

She stretched the money a long way, traveling alone in places few women dared go even with protection. She ventured to Hawaii, often riding and camping alone in remote regions only visited by the most intrepid adventurers. Sales of a book she wrote about her experiences, *Six Months in the Sandwich Islands*, provided the money needed to continue her travels.

Now, at age forty-two, she was thrilled to be in the Rocky Mountains, climbing peaks and mingling with outlaws.

Isabella knew the myths about Mountain Jim, many of which were developed through stories that were published in dime novels and Colorado newspapers. No one but Jim knew the truth, but a man named Evan Owens told a Denver newspaper reporter in 1886:

He was evidently driven away from home by grief he would never explain. . . . His bear fight took place in Middle Park in 1872. He started out one morning with his gun (a rifle) and a revolver, and a big knife which he always carried. When he got about a mile from camp he passed around the roots of a tree which had fallen to the earth. As he passed around the tree, Jim stepped right into a nest of Cinnamon bears. He was so close to them he couldn't shoot (his rifle), and only discharged one shot from his revolver, but with his big knife he killed them all three. Two hours later some of the boys from the camp found him lying unconscious among the three dead bears, one of which lay across his legs. Jim had come off as a conqueror, but one of his arms was broken, one eye was out, and his scalp torn loose and hanging over his face. He was torn and bitten over his body in a way that was dreadful to see.

Owens said Jim's mind was affected, yet, according to Isabella, it was a gentleman under the ragged clothing who asked politely to call on her the day she arrived in Estes Park. She rented a small, unchinked log cabin from Griff Evans, a Welshman who, with his family, had started a ranch that included accommodations for visitors. For $8.00 a day she had a bed, a washstand and bucket (in which the water routinely froze at night), enough blankets to keep her warm despite the snow that sifted through the gaps between the rough logs, and a skunk rooting about under the floor.

Isabella wanted to climb Long's Peak, a 14,700-foot mountain that towered over Estes Park. Mountain Jim said he would be her guide. The young students who had escorted her to Estes Park and Griff Evans joined the party. Everyone carried as much as possible for the three-day expedition.

The first part of the trip was arduous, but Isabella soon forgot the difficulties. "The ride was one series of glories and surprises, of 'park' and glade, of lake and stream, of mountains on mountains, culminating in the rent pinnacles of Long's Peak, which looked yet grander and ghastlier as we crossed an attendant mountain 11,000 feet high." Along the way Jim entertained Isabella with "a grace of manner which soon made me forget his appearance."

The small party camped about 3,000 feet below the summit. That night Isabella retired from the campfire to a bower of spruce. It was twenty degrees, and she huddled on a bed of pine boughs under several blankets with a saddle for a pillow and Jim's dog, Ring, at her back. She lay listening to wolves howling in the distance and watching the "notorious desperado, a red-handed man, sleeping as quietly as innocence sleeps" a few yards away beside the fire.

The next morning the ascent began, and Isabella later admitted to her sister that she never should have attempted it. "You know I have no head and no ankles, and never ought to dream of mountaineering; and had I known that the ascent was a real mountaineering feat I should never have felt the slightest ambition to perform it. As it is, I am only humiliated by my success, for 'Jim' dragged me up, like a bale of goods, by sheer force of muscle."

The party disagreed on which route to take, so Isabella and Jim went one way while the two young men and Griff Evans went another. At one point the steep ascent was so dangerous, the footing so uncertain, that Jim's dog would not proceed.

Awed by the summit, Jim and Isabella rested and studied the

rugged landscape. Then they began the long trek back down. In places it was so steep that Jim went before her, and Isabella used his broad shoulders as stepping stones.

Isabella said Jim reserved a brusque attitude for the two young students, but as soon as he and Isabella were alone on the trail, he became "gentle and considerate beyond anything, though I knew he must be grievously disappointed, both in my courage and my strength." She fell frequently among the boulders, snow, and patches of ice. At one point she hung perilously from the rocks, caught only by her dress. Jim used his hunting knife to cut her free; he made steps for her on his hands and knees, roped her to him with his lariat, and knelt to allow her to stand on his shoulders to reach the next level.

When at last they made it back to camp, Jim told the rest of the party they would stay put until morning. Isabella rolled up in her blankets, completely exhausted, and slept for a few hours until she was awakened by the cold. She got up and joined Jim at the campfire.

"The students were asleep not far off in their blankets with their feet toward the fire. 'Ring' lay on one side of me with his fine head on my arm, and his master sat smoking, with the fire lighting up the good side of his face, and except for the tones of our voices, and an occasional crackle and sputter as a pine knot blazed up, there was no sound on the mountain side."

As they sat beside the fire, Jim told Isabella of his early youth and of a "great sorrow which had led him to embark on a lawless and desperate life. His voice trembled, and tears rolled down his cheeks." Never in her life had Isabella met anyone like this outlaw. She loved Estes Park, and, maybe, she loved Rocky Mountain Jim Nugent. She described his dark side in brief sentences; for the rest her pen renders him almost heroic.

Mr. Nugent is what is called "splendid company." With a sort of breezy mountain recklessness in everything, he passes remarkably acute judgments on men and events; on women also. He has pathos, poetry and humor, an intense love of nature, strong vanity in certain directions, an obvious desire to speak in character, and sustain his reputation as a desperado, a considerable acquaintance with literature, a wonderful verbal memory, opinions on every person and subject, a chivalrous respect for women in his manner, which makes it all the more amusing when he suddenly turns round on one with some graceful raillery, a great power of fascination and a singular love of children. The children of this house run to him and when he sits down they climb on his broad shoulders and play with his curls.

Clearly fascinated, Isabella was not blind, and she often counseled him against drinking. "His magnificent head shows so plainly the better possibilities which might have been his. His life, in spite of a certain dazzle which belongs to it, is a ruined and wasted one, and one which asks of what good can the future have in store for one who has for so long chosen evil?"

What of Jim Nugent's thoughts about the woman whose courageous spirit belied her appearance, who never flinched from his scarred and ugly countenance, whose education and wit matched his own? The outlaw's actions perhaps give evidence of his feelings. Griff Evans and his family noticed that Jim, despite some long-standing grievances, was on his best behavior when he visited their cabin. The number of pleasant visits increased. Some said the amount of whiskey he consumed decreased, that the appearance of the virtuous lady called to something better, something almost forgotten in his dark soul.

Happy as Isabella was with her adventures in Estes Park, she recognized the dangers of romance. Later, she put into words the thoughts that troubled her: "He was a man that any woman might love, but no sane woman would marry." The parson's daughter decided to explore other parts of the Rockies.

Despite Jim's warnings of blizzards and Indian raids, Isabella set off in late October. Weeks passed. Traveling alone most of the time, she thought of Jim and knew her thoughts were dangerous. Darkness claimed Mountain Jim as soon as Isabella left Estes Park.

Through the wilderness Isabella trotted on her trusty mustang, Birdie, staying in whatever cabin or ranch house she happened upon. By November 6 she had ridden 150 miles over steep, snow-bound passes, crossing icy rivers at an elevation of approximately 9,000 feet. Except for a few chance meetings, she rode alone.

Nothing else she saw could compare to Estes Park. No one she met seemed half so fascinating as the one she'd left behind. She headed back to Muggins Gulch. The ride seemed endless. On the last day, riding in darkness, determined not to spend another night alone on the trail, she hurried ahead. "Finally the last huge range was conquered, the last deep chasm passed, and with an eeriness which craved human companionship, I rode up to Mountain Jim's den, but no light shone through the chinks and all was silent."

Dejected, Isabella rode on, the strange sounds of the night intensified by a loneliness she rarely knew. Suddenly a dog barked. Isabella called out to Ring. A moment later the dog's head and paws were braced on her saddle. Then a "musical voice" came to her from out of the darkness. Isabella's heart beat faster as Mountain Jim called out to her.

"The desperado was heartily glad to see me," she later wrote. Dismounting from her tired horse, Isabella walked with Jim 3 miles through the frosty night to her lodging.

Despite the warm welcome the outlaw became very grim soon after her return. "Mr. Nugent came in looking very black, and asked me to ride with him to see the beaver dams on Black Canyon. No more whistling or singing, or talking to his beautiful mare, or sparkling repartee. His mood was as dark as the sky overhead, which was black with impending snowstorm."

Isabella followed as Jim set a furious pace on the trail, racing ahead, cruelly spurring his mare until, abruptly reining in the horse, he turned a tormented face to Isabella. "You're the first man or woman who's treated me like a human being for many a year," he declared. "If you want to know how nearly a man can become a devil, I'll tell you now." Isabella at last learned the secrets of Jim's past, one of the "darkest tales of ruin" she'd ever heard or read.

His father, he said, was a British officer quartered in Montreal, Canada. His mother idolized her handsome, ungovernable son, and he tyrannized over her. Jim confessed to falling in love at seventeen. Passionate and intense, he insisted he would marry the girl, though he'd only seen her three times at church.

Jim's mother objected. To spite her he took to drink. Then the "angelic beauty" died. Maddened by the girl's death, he ran away from home and joined the Hudson's Bay Company. Even the "lawless life" of a trapper became too confining, so he quit and went roaming, and at about the age of twenty-seven became one of the famous U.S. government Indian scouts of the Plains.

Jim did not hesitate to tell Isabella of his bloody crimes. "Some of these tales I have heard before, but never so terribly told. Years must have passed in that service," Isabella told her sister, "till he became a character known through all the west, and much dreaded for his readiness to take offense, and his equal readiness with his revolver."

Women had found him attractive, Jim boasted. He would ride

through camps, a strong, handsome, broad-shouldered man with sixteen golden curls, each 18 inches long, hanging over his shoulders. That admiration had ended when a grizzly bear raked his face with wicked claws and left him mutilated, nearly dead.

Jim admitted to joining a gang of outlaws that raided in Kansas and other areas, but he despised himself for it. "He gets money, goes to Denver, and spends large sums in the maddest dissipation, making himself a terror, and going beyond even such desperados as Texas Jack and Wild Bill," she wrote to her sister, "and when the money is gone he returns to his mountain den, full of hatred and self-scorn, till the next time."

Snow had been falling unheeded as Jim poured out his tale. Finally, he guided Isabella to a sheltered place, turned to her once more, and admitted he could not give up whiskey. "Now you see a man who has made a devil of himself!" he cried. "You've stirred the better nature in me too late. I can't change. If a man were a slave, I am. Don't speak to me of repentance and reformation. I can't reform."

Jim then disappeared for two weeks. When he returned, he was haggard and pale, coughing severely. He invited the one woman who believed in him on a ride up the canyon of the Fall River. The scenery was grand, Isabella said, but the icy civility of her guide and his refusal to discuss the ride in the snowstorm and his agonized confession left her confused.

Was it all an act, she wondered, devised to mock her belief in the goodness of a soul, or was it a "genuine and unpremeditated outburst of passionate regret for the life he'd thrown away?" Deep in her heart, Isabella believed the desperado's confession came straight from the flickering light that struggled in his dark soul.

As winter continued, the weather worsened. The long separation from her sister began to weigh heavily on Isabella's spirits. Her funds frozen by a bank panic, she could not leave Estes Park. She could happily have spent the rest of her life there, but she knew her gentle sister, with whom she had a close relationship, needed her to make decisions about business and finances. Isabella was torn between devotion to Henrietta and this fascination with her own desperado.

At last Isabella faced the truth that if she did not leave soon, she would be imprisoned by snow until spring. On December 12 Griff Evans returned from Denver where he had exchanged a 100-pound note for Isabella. This money enabled her to leave for Denver. That day a knock came at her cabin door. "A gentleman came who I thought was another stranger, strikingly handsome, well dressed, and barely forty, with sixteen shining gold curls falling down his collar; he walked in and it was only after a second, careful look that I recognized in our visitor the redoubtable 'desperado.'"

The next morning Jim rode beside Isabella as she left Estes Park for Denver. Jim was a perfect gentleman all the way. Dressed in his best suit, he was an impressive figure that drew awed crowds. A dance was being held at the place where they spent the night. They didn't dance but sat quietly in the kitchen, for Isabella was afraid that access to liquor and pistols might tempt Jim from his good behavior. From eight in the evening until midnight, Jim and Isabella entertained each other. Occasionally, people peered in the kitchen windows for a glimpse of the notorious outlaw. "He repeated to me several poems of great merit which he had composed, and told me much more about his life. I knew that no one else could or would speak to him as I could, and for the last time urged upon him a reformation of his life, going so far as to tell him I despised a man of his intellect for being a slave to such a vice."

"Too late! Too late!" he sadly responded.

The mercury stood at twenty degrees below zero the next

morning as Jim escorted Isabella to the train station. There they met an Englishman named Fodder, also boarding the train. Isabella introduced the two men, not realizing that their polite handshake signaled the beginning of the end for her beloved outlaw.

Deep in amusing conversation with Fodder, Isabella hardly noticed when the train pulled away. When she looked back she saw Jim one last time, making his lonely way home. "I never realized that my Rocky Mountain life was at an end, not even when I saw 'Mountain Jim,' with his golden hair yellow in the sunshine, slowly leading the beautiful mare over the snowy Plains back to Estes Park . . . ."

By September of 1874 Isabella was back in England, and the relationship between Griff Evans and Mountain Jim had become very strained. Jim was resisting pressure from a wealthy British earl, Lord Dunraven, who had heard about Estes Park from Fodder. Dunraven wanted to turn the pristine area into a private hunting reserve. The deal would have benefited Griff Evans and his dude-ranch enterprise, but Jim was adamantly opposed. A violent quarrel between Jim and Dunraven's man, Haigh, took place, setting the stage for the final encounter.

Accounts of the fateful day vary. According to a later reconstruction published in the *Fort Collins Express*, Jim went to Evans's cabin "with blood in his eye and a gun on his shoulder." Haigh called a warning to Evans, who grabbed his shotgun. Evans fired twice, missing Jim with the first barrel and catching him in the face, neck, and head with the second load of pellets.

Wounded, Jim fell to the ground. But this was the man who had survived a fight against a trio of bears. Dr. George Kingsley, who was that day hunting at Estes Park, provided assistance and marveled at the "calm and plucky" attitude of his patient despite five wounds to the head.

One piece of lead shot had lodged in Jim's brain, but perhaps because the air in the high mountain valley was so pristine, no infection set in, and Jim's wounds apparently healed. Dr. Kingsley noted in his papers that the eye Jim had injured in the grizzly fight was still in place, but the bear's claw had scratched through the lid, causing an adhesion that the doctor was tempted to repair. He didn't, though, because he was sure that Jim would not survive with a piece of "Blue Whistler" in his brain.

Meanwhile, Griff Evans raced 30 miles to the nearest justice of the peace and swore out a warrant against his victim, charging Jim with assault. Jim later wrote an impassioned account of the course of justice for the newspaper.

> On the 14th ult. when the court sat at Fort Collins, and while
> I was still lying between life and death, the prosecuting attor-
> ney, without even coming to see me, although I had been lying
> within a mile of his residence for days, without hearing my
> story, goes before a grand jury and tries to have me indicted
> for assault with intent to kill, and who are the witnesses? Why,
> Evans, the would-be assassin, and his accessory, Haigh.

Isabella knew nothing of these incidents. Following her return to England she started writing a book about her adventures in Colorado. Yet her spirits plummeted. Unable to cast off her depression, she traveled to a clinic in Switzerland. There she meditated on her time in Estes Park and the outlaw she could neither reform nor forget. It was there that she saw the last of her gentleman outlaw in a vision so profound it later became known to the Society of Psychical Research in London. As clearly as she'd ever seen him in the pristine air of Estes Park, Mountain Jim appeared to her, sixteen golden ringlets shining on his shoulders, his one blue eye fixed on hers, but before she could reach out, his image faded.

Though she didn't know the cause, she was sure she understood the heartbreaking result. Thousands of miles away, at almost the same time, the piece of "Blue Whistler" from Griff Evans's shotgun finally stilled the heart of Rocky Mountain Jim.

The Bartender and the Soiled Dove

EARNEST MARKS AND ROSA MAY

Unattached females arrive in the boomtowns in a dead heat with the saloons. They entice men into small back rooms for amorous interludes, and split the fees with the saloon owners. I believe they are void of all human emotion and only love money.

—HARRISON PHILLIPS, *A MINER'S MEMOIRS*, 1852

Rosa May sat beside the cot of a dying miner and wiped the sweat off his feverish brow. She looked around his rustic, one-room cabin, past the sparse furnishings, and fixed her eyes on a tattered photograph of an elderly man and woman. "Those are my folks," the man weakly told her. "They're in Marshall County, Illinois. Where are your folks?"

The question stunned Rosa. No one ever asked about such things. No one ever asked her much at all. Conversation wasn't what men were looking for when they did business with her. Rosa glanced out the window at a couple of respectable, well-dressed women. They watched her through the clouded glass, pointed, and whispered. She knew what they were saying without hearing it.

Rosa was just one of a handful of "sporting women" living in Bodie, California, in 1900, and she knew what people thought of her. It used to bother her years ago, but not now. It was an occupational hazard she'd learned to live with.

"Don't you have people anywhere?" the miner asked.

COURTESY HELEN EVANS

Rosa May

Rosa dabbed the man's head with a cloth and smiled. "I don't know anymore," she answered. "If I did have they'd be back in Pennsylvania."

Rosa leaned back in her chair and sighed, her thoughts settling on her family. Rosa's parents were Irish—hard, strict people. Rosa had dreamt of the day she would be out of their puritanical household. She had left home in 1871, at the age of sixteen, and soon found there weren't many opportunities for a poor, petite, uneducated girl with brown eyes and dark, curly hair. She ended up in New York, hungry, homeless, and eager to take any job offered. The job offered was prostitution. Five years later she came west with other women of her trade, hoping to make a fortune off the gold and silver miners.

Prostitution was the single largest occupation for women in the West. Rosa hoped to secure a position at a posh brothel with crystal chandeliers, velvet curtains, and flowing champagne. The madams who ran such places were good to their girls. They paid them a regular salary, taught them about makeup, manners, and how to dress, and they only had to entertain a few men a night. If a high-class brothel wasn't available, Rosa could take a job in a second-class house and work for a percentage of the profits, turning as many tricks as she could each night. If all else failed, she could be a street walker or rent a "crib" at a boardinghouse. Cribs—tiny, windowless chambers—had oilcloths draped across the foot of the bed for customers in too big of a hurry to take off their boots.

She arrived in Virginia City, Nevada, in 1875 and went to work for a madam known as Cad Thompson. Cad was a widow who ran several parlor houses in town, including a three-story, brick structure called the "Brick House." Cad and Rosa became fast friends, confiding in one another and talking about meeting their Prince Charming. "Whores dream of falling in love, too," Cad frequently told Rosa.

In 1878 Rosa met a man she hoped would be her prince. His name was Earnest Marks. He was twenty-three, tall, well dressed, with a slight mustache. He told Rosa she was "handsomer in my eyes than anyone I know." The two found in one another what they most desired—human companionship and comfort.

Erni tried hard but had difficulties finding steady employment.

He worked doing whatever jobs he could find: mining, bartending, bill collecting. Most women would not have seen Erni as Prince Charming; he was a heavy drinker and a regular at brothels all over the area.

If Rosa had any thoughts that Erni would settle down with one woman, marry her, and save her from the life she led, Cad helped change her mind. Marriage didn't automatically mean that you would be living with your spouse or retire from prostitution, Cad told her. Oftentimes men who married prostitutes expected them to keep working. Cad believed Erni would expect no less from Rosa.

Rosa was not convinced. Erni always referred to her as his "little girl" and made her feel protected. She believed that if they were married, he would take care of her. But Erni Marks would never take Rosa May for his bride. The social stigma was too much for him to bear.

Rosa tried not to think about it as she sat in the dim room with the dying miner. She removed a pad of paper and a stump of a pencil from her oversized handbag and laid them on her lap. She had written letters for other Bodie miners suffering from pneumonia and was ready to write one more for the prospector next to her.

Rosa wrote letters constantly, often to families back East, telling them of the death of one of the girls working with her at the brothels. Many times her coworkers lost their lives at the hands of a customer, coworkers, or themselves, and Rosa felt an obligation to let their families know when their loved ones passed on. She believed they'd want to know, even if their loved ones were prostitutes.

Letters played an important part in Rosa and Erni's relationship. They exchanged many letters during the years they were together. Erni eventually left Virginia City and took a job in Gold Hill, a town some 20 miles away. Rosa and Erni wrote each other every three days. Rosa missed Erni terribly. He would travel to see her as often as time and money permitted, but in between visits she worried about his drinking and was jealous of his carousing. She knew he kept company with other prostitutes and madams. Despite her own profession and the countless men she entertained, she expected him to be monogamous.

Erni had a tremendous sexual appetite and found it impossible to live up to Rosa's standards. Many times Erni's letters to Rosa were written to ease her worries about his alcoholism and assure her of his true feelings.

February 2, 1879

Dear Rosa,
I was happy to get your letter today. I am being a good boy, love, and I shall continue to be. I am doing well, but am a little shaky. I suppose it is because I drink so little now, but I feel better for it and I look better too. No! Pet, I have not been with another. I have no interest in anyone, but you.
Love & kisses for my dearest Rosa.
Erni

But Erni was not faithful to Rosa. He had many lovers. Even if that hadn't been the case, he likely would have never publicly acknowledged his love for her. To admit being in love with a prostitute was scandalous, and Erni was afraid that neither he nor his family could endure the humiliation. Besides, his inability to hold down a job for any extended period of time had already left him with a poor self-image. He denied rumors that he and Rosa were a couple. When word of his denial would get back to Rosa, he would rush off another letter to reassure her of his love.

January 7, 1879

Dear Rosa,

You sweet, dear baby. I got your letter just fine. How could you believe that I might be moved by what others say about you and I. There's nothing to it. I don't let them bother me at all. You are my love.

Forever,
Erni

Rosa moved back and forth between parlor houses in Virginia City and Carson City, Nevada, following the gold and silver strikes. When the gold and silver were played out in both towns, fewer and fewer men visited Rosa, and some who did failed to pay. Rosa needed Erni to console her, but he was too busy with changes in his own life to think about her.

Erni moved to Bodie, California, to work for his brother in the wholesale liquor business. He curtailed his visits to see Rosa, who wrote him about how much this troubled her. She broke off their relationship and vowed never to write another word to him, but Erni's letter in response changed her mind.

April 17, 1879

My Darling Rosa,

Your letter sounds as though you feel hurt . . . I am sorry to see you feeling as you do. . . . I am sorry I was not on the train to meet you, but I hope you will think no harm in it and not feel hard toward your baby for I meant not to fool you and would not willingly disappoint my pet for any consideration. Why do you say goodbye? For today there is no hard task, no burden that I would not bear with grace, no sacrifice I could name or ask that were granted could I see your sweet face. Oh, Rosa how can you think for a moment that goodbye?

Always,

Erni

Rosa forgave Erni and took him back. Soon after, the letters again began to flow freely between the two lovers. Erni shared his feelings of insecurity with Rosa, and she shared her feelings of loneliness with him. They encouraged each other and held each other accountable for their misdeeds. Rosa chastised Erni for his drinking, and he would always apologize and promise to do better.

They also shared stories about their illnesses. Rosa suffered from chills and fever, a condition that originated when she lived in the cold, flimsy parlor houses in the East. Erni had gout and a venereal disease.

In 1891 Rosa moved to Bodie. Remote as it was, Bodie was still a booming gold town, and she thought business would be better, and she'd be close to Erni. She moved into a white house in the red-light district. She kept a neat brothel and listed her occupation with the census as "seamstress."

Erni was happy Rosa had moved to town. Under cover of darkness he would make his way back and forth from Rosa's home to the saloon where he worked. In the daylight Erni insisted that his relationship with Rosa was strictly professional.

Rosa turned to the miner and waited for him to begin dictating his letter. His eyes were wide open, but he wasn't breathing. Rosa gently covered his face with a sheet and blew out the candle sitting on the crude, wooden nightstand next to the bed. Rosa's gentle, giving spirit was the last kindness he would know.

Rosa herself eventually became sick with pneumonia and died in 1911 at the age of fifty-seven. Erni couldn't afford the monument he had promised Rosa he would put on her grave, and no one took up a collection to remember the gentle kindness of Rosa May. She was buried in the outcast cemetery, a simple wooden cross marking the spot.

Rosa's death left Erni heartbroken. Their romance had spanned thirty-five years. He was now an old, lame, near-penniless man with chronic prostate problems. He missed Rosa more than he could have imagined.

Erni lived out the rest of his days working in his bar. In 1919 Prohibition drove him out of the saloon and wholesale-liquor business. Relatives back East supported him until his death in 1928.

Legend has it that he asked to be buried next to his "little girl," Rosa, but he was buried in the Odd Fellow cemetery, far away from the outcast graveyard. In death as in life, Erni was publicly distant from Rosa May.

Author's note: All twenty-six of the letters Ernest Marks wrote to Rosa May can be found in the book *Rosa May: The Search for a Mining Camp Legend* by George Williams III (Carson City, Nev: Tree by the River Publishing, 1979).

The Journalist "Yellow Bird" and His Devoted Muse

JOHN ROLLIN RIDGE AND ELIZABETH WILSON

Oh lovely one that pined for me!
How well she soothed each maddened thought.
And from the ruins of my soul
a fair and beauteous fabric wrought.
—EXCERPT FROM JOHN ROLLIN RIDGE'S POEM "TO LIZZIE," 1852

The stagecoach carrying Elizabeth Wilson Ridge rattled and shook as it rolled along the rough trail that led to California. The gentleman passenger sitting across from her pushed his felt derby hat, knocked down over his eyes by the bumpy ride, up on his head. He looked up at Elizabeth and forced a smile. "I guess it's better than walking." Elizabeth nodded and turned toward the window, her thoughts settling on her husband awaiting her arrival.

John Rollin Ridge had left Elizabeth, their child, and their home in Fayetteville, Arkansas, in 1849 to strike it rich in the gold-fields of California. Elizabeth had been waiting patiently for three years for John to send for her. A letter he had sent his mother prompted Elizabeth to head west after him, leaving their baby in the care of her grandmother. John was ill. He was suffering from "billious fever," a condition that resulted in "ulceration of the bowels." His state was exacerbated because no family members were

Elizabeth Wilson

there to nurse him and tend to his needs. Elizabeth had in mind to rectify the situation. It was 1853, and thousands of pioneers were on their way west in hopes of striking it rich. Elizabeth tagged along with a pioneer family headed to San Francisco. She hoped her husband would still be alive when she arrived.

Elizabeth and John had met in Fayetteville several years before.

He had been attending law school in Connecticut but had returned to Arkansas because the climate in New England proved too cold. The two first became acquainted while he was studying Greek and Latin under a local missionary for whom Elizabeth worked. John was half Cherokee, and Elizabeth, who was part Native American herself, thought he was the handsomest man she had ever seen. John was just as taken by Elizabeth. In a letter to his cousin, he described his feelings for her: "There is a prettily shapely girl of about 16 or 17 years, who is very friendly and gives me a quantity of enjoyment in her company, whenever I get tired of dusty pages of legal technicalities."

John fell in love with Elizabeth's beautiful features, brilliant mind, and noble character. Elizabeth believed John to be a gifted writer and one of the brightest men in the country. The two were married in May of 1847. Elizabeth made John happy, but not happy enough to erase the tragic images from his past that haunted him.

John's father, Major John Ridge, was among the most powerful and wealthy of the eastern Cherokee in the early 1800s. John was born in 1827, a year that proved to be a most troublesome time for his people. The U.S. government had found gold on Cherokee land in Georgia and wanted the Cherokee moved off. Cherokee leaders were opposed to signing treaties with the U.S. government and refused to go. Major Ridge also opposed the tribe's removal, but for some reason, probably the hopelessness of the situation, he and a few other leaders changed their minds about negotiating with the federal government. They signed a treaty selling the Cherokee lands, an act many of the tribesmen considered treason. A death penalty was declared for the leaders who had signed the treaty.

On the morning of June 2, 1839, a group of tribesmen dragged Major Ridge from his bed and into the yard of his home and murdered him as eleven-year-old John, his mother, and all of his brothers and sisters watched. John's mother took her family to the comparative

CALIFORNIA HISTORICAL SOCIETY, FN-15881

John Rollin Ridge

safety of northwestern Arkansas. No matter how far away they went, John could not forget the heinous crime.

Even as an adult, he frequently dreamt of the scene and would awaken from his nightmares screaming and crying. Elizabeth would wipe the sweat from his brow and calm him down. She felt John's horror in the barbaric act just as deeply. John vowed to avenge his father's death. "There is a deep seated principle of revenge in me which will never be satisfied, until it reaches its object," he told Elizabeth. She stroked his head and promised to help him any way she could. She went with him to Oklahoma. There the two teamed up with several Ridge allies, all dedicated to punishing those who had murdered John's father.

John was an exceptional shot and had a talent with the bowie knife, but Elizabeth still worried for his safety. The Ridge warriors were a force to be reckoned with, successfully doing away with most of the men responsible for the assassination. Of the thirty-six tribesmen involved in the murder of Major Ridge, all but four were killed.

John's pursuit ended with an altercation with one of the four remaining murderers, Judge David Kell, who was instrumental in organizing the party that took Major Ridge's life. Judge Kell mutilated John's prized stallion, hoping to provoke John into a fight so that he could kill him. Indeed, the two men faced off, and when Kell advanced on John, John Ridge shot him dead, claiming self-defense. John doubted he would get a fair trial before the Cherokee court, so he fled to Missouri with his faithful Elizabeth.

The young couple set up house in Springfield, Missouri. In March of 1848 Elizabeth gave birth to a daughter they named Alice. John made a modest living for his family selling political articles to various newspapers and working in the county clerk's office. But the clerking job was a position that did not satisfy him.

Elizabeth was not surprised when news of the California Gold Rush arrived and John decided to join a company heading west. He kissed his bride and child goodbye and promised to send for them as soon as he could. Elizabeth hoped John would find peace in California. "Your father is still tormented," she told Alice. "Always his path is a trail of tears."

John was enamored with the West. He loved the wide-open spaces and endless possibilities. He spent much of his first three years in the Gold Country mining and market hunting near a camp called Whiskey Town, but he did not find success in either endeavors. By the autumn of 1853, he had decided to abandon mining altogether. In a letter to his beloved Elizabeth, he expressed disappointment in his circumstances: "It has been a series of bad luck here. I have worked harder than any slave. All to no purpose. I have tried the mines, I have tried trading, I have tried everything, but to no avail, always making a living, nothing more!

John accepted another clerking job, this time in Yuba, California. He also wrote for a New Orleans newspaper, describing the overland journey to the mines. He wrote under the moniker of "Yellow Bird", the name given to him when he was a boy by his fellow Cherokee tribesmen. By early 1853 he was also a regular contributor of verse and sketches to a San Francisco magazine called *The Pioneer*.

By the time Elizabeth reached John in California, he was close to death. Her comforting spirit and round-the-clock care saw John through the worst of it and helped him get back on his feet. John had missed Elizabeth's calming influence. "You bless me with your love, dear Lizzie," he told her. "How could I have been apart from you for so long?" Once John was on the mend, Elizabeth returned to the East to get their daughter. She traveled back to California via the Isthmus of Panama. John was waiting for her and Alice in San Francisco, where the three had a tearful reunion.

Elizabeth encouraged John to hone his writing skills. He began selling more of his poems, finding his voice penning sonnets about the beauty of California. Elizabeth noticed a change in her husband: His temperament seemed less volatile, and she attributed the transformation to the time he was spending writing. He still agonized over his father's murder but used a pen and paper to shoo away those lingering demons.

In the summer of 1854, the notorious bandit Joaquin Murieta disappeared, but not before capturing John's imagination. John decided to write a book about Joaquin's exploits. He had empathy for this desperate Mexican driven to a life of crime after his fiancée was killed and he was forced off his land. John's book, *The Life and Adventures of Joaquin Murieta, the Celebrated California Bandit*, was a literary success. Unfortunately John Ridge never benefited from it financially. The publisher went bankrupt, and John never received any royalties from the sales. The book, however, did help John secure newspaper editing jobs. He was the first editor for such papers as the *Sacramento Bee*, the *Marysville Democrat*, and the *Grass Valley Union*.

Elizabeth and John settled in Grass Valley, California, and remained there for more than fifteen years. Their daughter, Alice, was married in the parlor of their family home. Elizabeth doted on their child and supported her husband's efforts as an outspoken political journalist. The couple was well thought of in the community.

At the age of thirty-nine, John's health began to fail. He suffered from a condition known as "softening of the brain." The disease advanced throughout the spring and summer of 1867 and in the last two weeks of September, John Ridge was disabled and bedridden. Tended by Elizabeth, he remained in a feverish state, often lapsing into incoherence.

On October 5, 1867, John Rollin Ridge died. His obituaries were lengthy and for the most part laudatory, even from rival newspapers. He left behind a legacy of fine writing, and Elizabeth worked to perpetuate his gift. In 1868 she published a volume of his poems. She cherished all his work but favored the poems he had written for her. In an excerpt from his poem "To Lizzie," written in

1852, John described just what it was about his wife that inspired him: "The beauteous one before me stands / Pure spirit in her down-cast eyes, / And like twin doves her folded hands."

Elizabeth Wilson Ridge lived until 1905. Her body was laid to rest next to her husband's at the Greenwood Cemetery in Grass Valley.

The Gallant Groom and the Bereaved Bride

ANSEL EASTON AND ADELINE MILLS

With clasped hands we talked to each other of our dear, dear friends, of our brief happiness together, and our hopes for the future.
—ADELINE EASTON'S JOURNAL, SEPTEMBER 1857

On August 20, 1857, an elegantly dressed wedding party marched down a busy San Francisco thoroughfare behind a beautiful horse-drawn carriage carrying the bride and groom. The procession followed the carriage to the wharf on Vallejo Street and cheered the couple as they alighted from their ride.

The bride, Adeline Mills Easton, was a petite, vivacious woman with large, dark eyes. Adeline's family were leaders in finance and industry. Her brother, Darius Ogden Mills, established his fortune investing in banks, railroads, and other businesses associated with gold and silver mines. The groom, Ansel Easton, was a distinguished man with short, dark hair and a neatly trimmed goatee. He had emigrated to California in early 1850 and amassed a fortune selling furnishings to the new steamship lines. He raised thoroughbred horses on his 1,500-acre estate south of San Francisco.

The pair hurried up the gangplank leading to their honeymoon steamer, pausing only a moment to wave to the entourage below. Their arms were filled with swinging baskets of wedding gifts and hampers of wine and sweet cakes. Ansel gently kissed his wife and escorted her aboard the ship.

The S.S. *Sonora* left San Francisco that afternoon carrying the newlyweds and 398 other passengers on the first leg of their journey to New York via Panama. Adeline and Ansel were very much in love and spent the fourteen days enjoying each other's company, exploring the ship, and meeting new friends. It was an unforgettable experience for the couple. Adeline recalled in her journal that "the voyage to the Isthmus was one of long delight, with smooth sailing waters, sunny skies, and a joyous congenial company."

Adeline and Ansel arrived in Panama on September 3, 1857. Arm in arm they made their way to the Panama Railroad Station to be transported to the vessel that would take them the rest of the way to New York. Cargo and mail were awaiting the travelers. The couple pored over letters and telegrams from friends and family back home wishing them a happy life. The two had no doubt that they would be together always.

The newlyweds boarded the S.S. *Central America* and stood on the promenade deck holding each other and thinking of their promising future as the United States mail-ship pushed away from the dock on the way out to sea. The Eastons were quite impressed with their first-class stateroom aboard the steamer. It contained three berths, one above another, and it had a cushioned locker, mirror, toilet stand, washbowl, water bottles, and glasses. The floors were covered with carpet, and the berths were screened with outer silk curtains and inner white linen curtains.

William Lewis Herndon was the captain of the *Central America*. Captain Herndon had achieved national fame in 1851 for leading the first scientific expedition down the Amazon River. Passengers enjoyed talking with Herndon and listening to his exciting tales of adventure. Captain Herndon often invited certain guests

Adeline Mills

to dine with him during the evening meal. The Eastons were among those chosen few. They were captivated by the Captain's stories of the discoveries he had made on his amazing jungle mission. On September 8 Adeline noted her favorable impression of William Herndon in her journal. "The Captain was a most interesting and delightful man and we enjoyed dining with him very much."

The newlyweds returned to their cabin that night, retelling the Captain's tales of eating monkey meat and surviving attacks from hostile natives, but just as they and the other passengers were settling into their cabins for the night, a violent wind began to toss the ship about. By morning a storm had set in. Adeline was anxious, but Ansel assured her that the *Central America* was sturdy. Ansel, along with several other fellow travelers, believed the storm would pass within twenty-four hours.

Adeline and Ansel remained in their stateroom, waiting. They sat quietly, listening to the sounds of the waves pounding against the sides of the ship and the moans of those suffering from seasickness. The storm continued to rage on into the night. A steward came to the Eastons' room to ask if they needed something to eat. Adeline was too ill to even think about food.

By morning the *Central America* had been blown well off its course. High seas broke over the bow, sprayed across the decks, and splashed against the staterooms. Ansel was beginning to have his doubts about the vessel's stability, but he kept his apprehensions to himself. As it grew dark, the sea breaking over the steamer spilled into the staterooms, forcing some of the first- and second-class passengers, including the Eastons, to abandon their cabins. On September 11 Adeline recalled, "The vessel suddenly careened to one side, and, looking toward our port hole, I noticed that it was entirely under water."

Waves exploded high into the air, and salt spray mixed with rain drenched the pair as they made their way to a relatively dry section of the ship.

The storm continued on, and the ship was further tossed about. When the steam pumps became too flooded to work, male passengers and crew members were ordered to go to work bailing. Adeline wanted to stay with her husband and help, but Ansel wouldn't allow it. She sat, waiting and wondering, as he went off to

bail with the others. He would occasionally break away from his
work and sit with his bride and hold her.

Adeline was scared for Ansel. She was afraid he might be
washed overboard by the waves. She blamed herself for the state in
which they found themselves. "Ansel, if you hadn't married me, you
wouldn't be in all this trouble," she cried.

"If I knew it all beforehand, I should do the same again," he
assured her.

"If it is our time, we will go down together, hand in hand," she
replied.

"But, until all hope is past, we must work," Ansel told her.

Adeline resigned herself to that idea, let her husband go back
to work, and joined the other women huddled on the port side of
the main cabin, bracing themselves against the relentless storm.

The following morning brought no relief—the sea had almost
swamped the ship. The passengers had very little to eat, because the
storm had blown the ship off course and away from the stops that
needed to be made in order to resupply the ship with provisions.
Bread was all that was left, and that was soaked by the water. The
men had been bailing for thirty hours and were exhausted and hungry. Adeline suddenly realized how she could help.

"I thought of the hampers in our stateroom, and with great
difficulty reached the room and brought out the boxes of biscuits
and some wine." Adeline remembered in her journal. "As I passed
among the men they eagerly took the crackers and wine, only stopping long enough to eat them and then going on with the work of
bailing. All night at intervals I went the rounds until everything we
had was used."

As night again set in, there was a break in the storm, but it was
short-lived. Rain clouds thickened again, and hurricane-force winds
tossed more seawater onto the ship. The vessel was now sinking.

On August 29 the ship *Marine* had departed Cuba, bound for Boston. The ship was now running parallel to the *Central America* and was also working hard to stay afloat in the storm. When Captain Herndon spotted the *Marine's* sails he ordered the signal guns fired at once and a flag of distress hoisted. The captain of the *Marine* saw the brilliant flash from the guns and signaled to Captain Herndon that his ship would assist the *Central America*.

Herndon ordered the lifeboats launched and all women and children on deck. The heaving sea immediately overtook two of the lifeboats, rendering them useless. With great difficulty the women and children were lowered by ropes from the deck into the three remaining lifeboats.

Adeline didn't want to leave Ansel. "I can't go without you," she cried. Ansel convinced her that she had to go and promised that he would follow soon. With tears streaming down her face, she kissed her husband and told him that she would pray for him. Adeline noted that incident in her journal on September 12, 1857: "In a moment I was swinging from the deck, and when a swell brought the little boat underneath, the rope was lowered and I dropped to the bottom of the boat. It was a dreadful moment. Just then the contents of one of the barrels they were bailing with came down on my head, completely drenching me. Ansel threw the coat he was wearing to me."

The storm raged on. It took two and a half hours for the lifeboats to reach the *Marine*. The captain welcomed the cold, weary passengers with cheering words of encouragement, but Adeline feared they had left one sinking ship for another. The lifeboats were sent back to the *Central America*, and the captain hurried the women and children down to the cabins. Adeline refused to go. "My only thought was for my husband, and I could not be prevailed upon to join the others below," she remembered.

I watched the boats which had returned to the sinking ship.
Soon one came near enough to see the people who were in
her. Surely he would be there, but no. However, close behind
came another boat, and hope was centered on her. Alas,
another disappointment, and then with anxious heart and
choking fear I saw a third boat come close to the ship and in
it was not the one I longed to see. It was growing dark and
the boatmen refused to go back again to the ship. I put my
face down in my hands, too wretched to speak, reproaching
myself that I had not stayed with him, regretting that I had
not defied the Captain and all when they ordered us to leave.

Adeline watched the *Central America* sink lower and lower into
the sea. Captain Herndon took his position in the wheelhouse and
fired rockets downward, the usual signal that a ship was sinking rapidly. Adeline recorded the heartbreaking scene in her journal: "A
rocket shot out obliquely. The lights disappeared beneath the waves
and all the world grew dark for me."

The ship plunged deep into the water and disappeared from
sight. Some men fought their way to the surface and were floating
about on wooden planks. Bodies floated in the water, bobbing up
and down like corks.

The *Marine* arrived in Norfolk, Virginia, six days later.
Adeline's heart was so heavy over the loss of her husband she could
barely bring herself to think about what she would do once ashore.
A harbor pilot boarded the *Marine* and brought news about forty-
nine other survivors who had been picked up by the ship *Empire
City*. The pilot knew none of them by name. Adeline later wrote, "I
felt very sad and downcast and scarcely spoke for I knew my hopes
were soon to be realized or I must yield to despair."

The *Empire City* headed into Norfolk Bay carrying men who

had survived the sinking. As the ship approached the *Marine*, now moored at the dock, the women aboard realized the men lining the rail were some of those left behind on the *Central America*. They began weeping and laughing hysterically, frantically searching the faces of the men, hoping to recognize one of them.

As soon as the *Empire City* weighed anchor, the crew was mobbed by frantic women from the *Marine* trying to get to their loved ones. The ship's captain asked to see Adeline Easton. She nervously came forward, tears in her eyes. "Your husband is awaiting your arrival, Missus Easton. He was among the men rescued by the bark."

"I scarcely knew what to do," Adeline recalled. "A number of ladies threw their arms around me and kissed me while the captain and other gentlemen, and even the rough sailors, shook me heartily by the hand and congratulated me for the safety of my dear husband."

Adeline and other tattered, shipwrecked survivors headed to the National Hotel, the official base for the ill-fated passengers. Adeline burst into the hotel expecting to find Ansel, but he wasn't there. He had grown impatient waiting for her to reach him and set out to meet up with her at the ship. The two had passed each other in the night.

Adeline took a seat in the hotel's grand parlor and waited. After a while Ansel returned and found his bride of four weeks sitting by a fire. The couple embraced without saying a word. Adeline recalled, "We wept together as well as rejoiced and for several nights after we could neither of us sleep, so vivid were the scenes before us that passed through."

Ansel and Adeline headed to New York on the *Empire City*. Friends and family were there to greet them once they landed. The pair had shared an experience that changed their lives and would strengthen their marriage. They would retell their story over and over again with sadness and grateful hearts.

"My watch, my beautiful ring, wedding presents, and many other things I valued were all lost," noted Adeline. "Though I shall never behold them again I still have the blessed privilege of preserving them in memory and I have my darling husband, the most precious jewel of all."

After a couple of weeks in New York, the Eastons returned to their home in California. They had two children, a boy and a girl. Eleven years after the sinking of the *Central America,* Ansel was thrown from one of his racehorses and died. Adeline went on, eventually raising her and Ansel's grandchildren after their daughter passed away giving birth to her third child. Adeline never remarried. She died at the age of eighty-six.

John Bidwell

The General and the Spiritual Spinster

JOHN BIDWELL AND ANNIE KENNEDY

I retired to the privacy of my room and there fervently prayed, "Oh Lord, give the General a wife worthy of him—some other person. Oh Lord, do not do it—let me be his wife."

—ANNIE ELLICOTT KENNEDY

Pages of the letter slipped from Annie's nerveless grasp. Numb with shock, she pressed a hand to her heart. Her knees gave way, and she sank to the floor. Blindly staring at the scattered pages, she drew in a deep, shaking breath.

"I never could marry unless I loved, and I never loved till I came here, and then with an intensity that seemed to me to equal if not surpass any tale of fiction." Words written in the strong hand of General John Bidwell seemed to jump off the page and dance before her eyes. "I love you Annie, more than all the world beside." Closing her eyes in anguish, she prayed for forgiveness, for assistance, for the light of the Redeemer to show her the way.

This declaration of love was not what she had intended.

Burned into her brain, the words in the letter repeated themselves: "These emotions have been growing in me from the time I first saw you. The more I saw the more I wanted to see you. I thought of nothing but you during all my tour in Europe."

Annie felt almost ill. Her father, a superintendent of the national census, had invited General Bidwell, the congressman from

California, to dinner a year ago! General Bidwell had been a frequent visitor to the house after that, but Annie had naturally assumed political interests had brought him so often to her house in Washington, D.C.

Just yesterday she'd seen him at church, and no hint of these dangerous emotions had shown. Could it be that the religious verses she'd sent him had been misinterpreted? She'd copied them the night before, but not, she thought in horror, with such a result in mind. She was devoted to her church and family; marriage was definitely not in her plans.

Quickly, needing an end to the matter at once, she dashed off a few lines of refusal, folded the note into an envelope, and sent it to the congressional office where General Bidwell spent his days. Then, turning to the one source of comfort and mercy that never failed her, she picked up her Bible and prayed for guidance.

Later that day she realized the abrupt answer she'd sent lacked the Christian kindness she tried always to practice. That evening, January 2, 1867, she wrote a second answer to the shocking letter.

The next night, General John Bidwell opened the envelope with a shaking hand. She'd refused him once. Had she changed her mind? Everything he wanted in life hung in the balance.

He had thought long and hard about the large difference in their ages. He knew of the strong family bond that knitted together Annie Kennedy's family, knew he had nothing but his own strength to take its place if she agreed to marry him.

With few qualms he'd left his kinfolk behind when he set out to explore the West. He'd been nineteen, with an eye for adventure and a dream of finding good farmland. Now he was forty-six, with 25,000 acres of prime ranch land in California. He needed a wife, but until he'd met Annie Kennedy, no woman had attracted his interest.

Annie Kennedy

Annie was the one thing he considered necessary to make
Rancho del Arroyo Chico a home, the one thing he had to have to
center his life. The paper crackled as he unfolded Annie's second letter and read the words.

Wednesday, January 2, 1867

My dear friend,
Words are quite inadequate to express the varied emotions
produced by the perusal of your letter. I was wholly ignorant
of your thoughts of me. That you entertained warm friend-
ship for me I believed, as your numerous kind attentions
attested, and it was pleasant to think thus, as we all esteemed
you highly, and enjoyed your society, but it never occurred to
me that you thought of me as you assure me you do. Do not
think me ungrateful if obliged to write that which may grieve
you.

She hadn't changed her mind. John's heart sank.

Be assured I am deeply grieved myself. Grieved that I should
be the cause of pain to you. The lines I sent you this morning
were too abrupt, but it seemed right not to mislead you.

There was more, several pages, but he could not make himself
continue yet. He knew she would pray for him, and he was grateful,
but prayer had not proved to him the existence of that which Annie
believed with every particle of her being.

There lay the root of the problem. If he had the unquestioning
faith in Christian teachings that Annie did, perhaps the answer
would be different. Yet he could not lie about something that had

troubled his pragmatic mind for years. John knew that his faith in himself and his comrades and a vague belief that God would guide their efforts could not compare with Annie's entire life of devotion, prayer, and good works.

Bending again to the letter, John looked for a ray of hope. "So many of my views and actions are peculiar," she wrote, "and questioned even by my Christian friends, that my resolution has always been not to impose them on any one who could not understand them. This decision, with much prayer, has enabled me to control my affections, and upheld me in the hour of temptation."

Did that mean she might be just the slightest bit tempted? John read and reread the letter, sensing the turmoil his proposal had created. Annie was terrified. Yet her kind heart required she assuage the pain her first brusque refusal had caused.

A note to Annie the next day encapsulated his thoughts. "I try to act as if God were looking down on me constantly. The only refuge from worldly cares seems to be with you. I will try to see you often while I stay in Washington. But, Annie, unless you tell me your heart and hand are betrothed to another I shall live in hope as long as life shall last."

John's term in the Thirty-ninth Congress was drawing to a close. In March he would return to California. He'd been asked to run for Congress again but had declined. He thought he might be nominated for governor of California.

A few days later Annie wrote to him again, earnestly sharing her deepest spiritual beliefs and confessing her own difficulties in trusting Christian teachings and in opening her heart to spiritual love. She entreated him to think of her only as one who had prayed constantly for him for a week past. He frowned at the closing lines. "I must not write again, as comments are being made on my seclusion." Clearly, she had not recovered fully from the shock of his proposal.

He could not take it back, would not, but he wished somehow to ease her distress.

He knew how easily her strength could be depleted. She was less than 5 feet tall, with a tiny frame and a too-willing heart, and the constant social demands of her position and the good works she insisted on performing sometimes sent her to bed with neuralgia.

He saw her at church. He bought a pincushion at a church fund-raiser, earning her gratitude for the $50 he'd bid. He'd have emptied his pockets for another of her smiles. The short conversation they'd managed left him unsatisfied, but he could not subject her to idle talk lest his attentions become too noticeable.

A month sped past, bringing his departure closer. On February 22, with fewer than thirty days to win her heart, John pressed his luck and wrote Annie again of his deepest feelings. "The flight of time is rapid and inevitable. One thing is evident—we must know each other better—our relations be more intimate, or soon part never perhaps to meet again. But I cannot endure such a thought."

To advance his courtship would require Annie's permission to tell her parents of his proposal, but Annie forbade it. Still, he wrote again.

> I have thus far lived alone amid the turmoil of worldly cares, but it has been an unnatural life. Instead of having an Angelic being to love and cherish, business engrossed all my mind. I desire to return to California changed in habits and purposes and lead a different and better life. If I go there I fear that I may fall back into the same dull, aimless routine, unless my resolves are supported by a change of life—from a single to a wedded life.
>
> I do not want a companion to take care of me, for I can take care of myself, but I want one to depend on me, to lean on me for protection and support. The more slender and frail, the more I would delight to protect, cherish and adore her.

And in all this wide world there is to me only one such being, but one whom I can and do love—and that is you, Annie. You fill my thoughts by day and often through sleepless nights.

Knowing that his passion might terrify Annie anew, he once more asked if he might continue their correspondence, telling her that it was ultimately her decision. Annie's prayers had been constant for the large, commanding man who seemed somehow to have mistaken the needs of his soul for the worldly passion of the mind and heart. She had vowed never to marry. At twenty-six she had felt that she was safely past the afflictions of youthful desires. All she wanted was to continue her Sabbath classes at the mission deep in the poorest part of the nation's capital. She prayed for guidance.

On March 1, 1867, with only twenty days left before he departed from Washington, John carefully responded to a letter Annie had sent dashing his hopes again. What she'd written led him to believe she had already pledged herself to someone else. Annie was stricken with guilt and quickly wrote another letter admitting that no such promises had been made.

Hope soared anew in John, but his departure was drawing very close. On the nineteenth of March, Annie again tried to clarify her position. "How strange it is that sometimes words seem so inadequate to express the depth of feeling which we would convey, and then again so magnify a simple sentence. It seems my hand is doomed to wound where it longs to heal." She explained, however, that she did not intend to marry, ever.

The next morning, unaware that John's ship was to sail on the following day, she described the depth of her most spiritual beliefs and her efforts to find peace. John arrived for a brief visit, his correct and congenial behavior reminding her of the worth of the man for whom she prayed daily. Their parting loomed irrevocably.

That night John put pen to paper, tore up the letter, and wrote anew on Thursday, the day of his departure. "The future to me is all gloom." He knew she did not want to hear of his worldly love, yet he could not put it out of his heart. She'd told him not to wait for her to change her mind. "I am not waiting," he wrote, "but I am persuaded that I shall never marry unless I loved . . . It is well, doubtless, that I am going away. I shall then cease to annoy you. Now, Annie, I bid you an affectionate good-by. I shall try to meet you in heaven."

Thursday morning, after receiving John's final goodbye, Annie realized her mistake. Unable to speak to him frankly, unable even to contemplate such a thing, she again resorted to pen and ink.

> It is useless to attempt a reply to your epistle of this morning.
> My heart is too full, but I must prepare a few lines to place in
> your hand if it can possibly be done. . . . I have felt as you do,
> bewildered by the apparent want of fitness in these matters,
> but by the grace of God I knew where to find relief. My feel-
> ings were not, of course, to be compared with yours, for I saw
> my danger before it became a portion of my being, and God
> stilled the coming tempest before it became one. I might say,
> why does God not change his heart, why should I happen to
> like one who I dare not think more of than a dear friend?

John made a farewell call on the family and then left for New York. Almost immediately, Annie began to worry about the last unguarded note she'd sent. Had she confessed too much? Realization that an entire country would soon separate her from John caused her anxiety to increase. Transcontinental mail arrived and departed every two weeks, and the trip to California by ship took at least three weeks. Any misunderstandings, and there must be many, she thought, would take months to resolve.

Guilt ate at her, too, for she had conducted secret correspondence with a man. A partial confession to her mother did not relieve her conscience. She prayed for guidance to do what was right. She knew she could get one more letter to John before he sailed from New York harbor.

John arrived in New York on a cold and gloomy day. At his hotel on Fifth Avenue, he read and reread Annie's last letter. He poured his heart into prayer and briefly felt a calmness descend. But by the time he'd concluded his business, depression had returned. No letter arrived from Annie, though he paid a man to wait in the rain for one until the last minute.

John arrived in California in late April 1867. He was nominated for governor, and on Sunday, June 2, he wrote Annie that he would be very involved in politics. "Yesterday our primary elections were held. I have not heard a word as to the result . . . If I am defeated, it will be trickery to which I persistently refuse to descend. Friends have appealed to me, saying 'money must be used—if we expect to win we must have money in San Francisco, otherwise we shall lose the city . . .'" But John had refused the money, the influence peddling, and all political deals. If nothing else, he would try to stay true to the ideals of the woman he loved, though he might never see her again.

John's long letter to Annie on June 18 contained just a few sentences about the election. "The great political struggle is over, and I was defeated for governor—defeated while 19 out of 20 of the Union people of the state were in my favor—defeated by money, fraud and the vilest trickery ever known to political contests on this coast—defeated because I would not stoop to corruption." That election led to reorganization of the Republican Party in California. John was encouraged to run again, but he declared that once was enough.

The slow passage of days between transcontinental mail deliveries tortured Annie, for all she could do was study earlier letters and try to read between the lines. Daringly, she wrote again.

> Many a time I have concealed myself to weep when teased about it being my duty to marry. Oh how can I ever leave my home, and those of whose affection and kindness I am sure, for one almost a stranger, in comparison. It seemed like launching out to sea, in a dark uncertain night; there might be a great beauty and peace, but there might be desolating storms.
>
> I do not fear you, General. Under all circumstances I believe you would be gentle and kind. I could trust you, unhesitatingly, could confide myself to your care with no misgivings, so it is not because I fear you nor could not trust you, but because there are great obstacles in the way.

For the man who had left home at the age of nineteen with nothing but a pocketknife and less than $100 and then, two years later, led a party of emigrants across the western desert and over the rugged barrier of the Sierra Nevada, Annie's "great obstacles" seemed small. But he was careful to restrain the thrill of hope her words created, as he wrote the following:

> Now Annie, I am going to refer to what you say that you once thought of notifying me in case you should change your mind (about marrying me), but you would not do so for fear it would unsettle my mind. Now I assure you, it will not unsettle my mind. Can you not make me the promise now? That you will advise me in case you should change your mind? I will make every promise.

He promised to send her to visit her family whenever she wished and to provide for her in every way. "You would reign supreme in my heart. We would be one . . . You overwhelm me when you say you could trust yourself to me unhesitatingly. I can only promise all my heart in return."

Although Annie read to her mother from John's letters, she carefully edited out the subject of marriage. Confessing and then having to talk about "just how much I care for another" she considered unendurable.

Finally a letter arrived in Chico that lifted John's spirits. Believing that Annie had at long last given him permission to inform her parents of his feelings, John composed a letter to her father. After several long paragraphs he finally dove into the heart of the matter: "I must come to the main question, the subject of deepest moment to me and on which seem to hang all my future prospects." He explained his admiration and respect for Annie and then asked the vital question, "Can you consent to confide her to me?"

John didn't know that Annie had already written to retract permission to speak to her father of marriage, but John wouldn't receive that letter for a month. He believed that progress had been made in their long-distance love affair, until the late-arriving letter threw him into cold despair. Meanwhile, on October 7, Annie wrote again of her desire, but at the last moment she thrust the letter into an envelope marked "Not to be opened until permission shall have been given, expect in case of my death or your serious illness. But to be returned to me when requested."

On November 16 John penned a careful reply. Despite his desire to tear open the mysterious envelope, he restrained himself and assured Annie he would do exactly as she had asked. But the temptation soon became too great and he opened the forbidden letter. It read:

What would you think were I to say that your naughty, trying, vexing, obstinate and otherwise culpable friend, con-
cludes, on mature reflection, to repent these graceless traits,
and commending herself to your clemency and affection, ask
your forgiveness?

Yes, it is ever so, General; I find myself conquered—by
your constancy, and the many noble traits of character developed by time and circumstances, as also by a mysterious prov-
idence which constrains me to make this confession. Mama
assures me of Papa's and her cordial approval of our marriage,
and even insists she believes I have loved you from the very
first!!! Do you believe it?

John immediately wrote:

Oh Annie. My Dearest Annie—What shall I say? After writing you today I read again your little note enclosed with the
missile 'not to be opened' . . . I suspected more than I can now
write, and I could not help opening the forbidden charge. It
was not sealed. The temptation was too great!!! . . . I am yours
and you are mine!

John began planning to leave for Washington, D.C., to claim
the bride he had dreamed of for more than a year. But, believing
that he had not yet opened the forbidden envelope, Annie sent John
another letter that told of her deep doubts and anxiety. Receipt of
this letter crushed John's dreams. On December 17, still in Chico, he
confided his confusion, "Have I committed an unpardonable offense?
I have been acting upon the idea that you had already consented to
give yourself away, that for better or worse we were to run the race
of life together . . . Why do you hesitate?"

Finally Annie wrote: "I write you this morning to give permission to open the 'sealed' note referred in your last letter, and to say that it may be considered my final decision." She explained that the note had been written with the intention that it be read as soon as it arrived in Chico. Before it could be mailed, however, Annie's mother advised her to wait until her father had been informed. So, in a halfway measure, she enclosed the letter in an unsealed envelope, instructed John to leave it unread, and sent it off, not realizing the confusion that would ensue.

The postal system caused one more difficulty for the lovers. Annie and her mother started planning a late-spring wedding. Annie sent three letters to John with a program of events laid out, but John set sail before those letters reached him. Consequently, he arrived on the East Coast the first week of February, long before he was expected, months before Annie had intended.

Excitement and dread filled Annie when she learned that John had arrived in New York. They exchanged a flurry of letters and notes. He wanted to be married as quickly as possible; she held out for a spring wedding. The confusion and fear of the future, of entrusting herself to a man she had not seen in so long, combined with the stress of preparing a wedding, exhausted Annie's strength. She begged for delay.

In a long, carefully worded letter on March 27, John explained the needs of his ranch, the vagaries of California weather, and the importance of taking care of the business that had suffered during his term in Congress.

> I am trying to come to the point, gently, very gently, because I
> do not wish to shock your delicate nerves. How shall I do it?
> It is this—do not—or rather, Dearest Annie, promise me not
> to ask for a delay in our departure until the 1st of May. I

write this note very reluctantly, for fear you may intimate again a postponement.

On April 16, 1868, John Bidwell and Annie Kennedy were married at her family home. President Andrew Johnson, General Ulysses S. Grant, General William T. Sherman, and a host of other notable guests attended the wedding. The newly married couple departed aboard the *Rising Star* on April 24, headed for a new life together in California that lasted thirty-two years and set a new standard for a partnership based on mutual faith in themselves, in each other, and in God.

John and Annie laid out extensive and productive orchards at Rancho Chico, with Annie carrying the surveyor's flag for her husband. The fruits of their labor won gold medals at the state fair John had helped establish. They also set up a refuge at Rancho Chico for Indians who were treated badly and nearly exterminated in the state.

Together, they worked for temperance, women's rights, and equal opportunity and justice regardless of race, creed, or color. John employed Chinese workers, and under pressure to fire them during a surge of anti-Chinese sentiment, he refused to do so.

Together, they donated land for the town of Chico, and for schools and churches. (At present, Bidwell Park is a green haven comprising hundreds of acres in the center of the now-thriving city.)

Together, John and Annie put into practice the basic principles of their beliefs, with love leading the way.

The Irishman and the Copper Queen

Marcus Daly and Margaret Evans

He came to Utah and did some mining in different parts of the state and it was here that he made the greatest strike of his life—he found and won the wife that was his life and light even until his final call.

—C. C. Goodwin, *Goodwin's Weekly*

Margaret Daly smiled at her new husband as the stagecoach jolted over the ruts and stones littering the road to Ophir, Utah. They were miles from Salt Lake City, where they had been married. A spring breeze cooled the air, and fluffy white clouds moved across the sky.

The bumpy road wound through the valley and past Tooele and Stockton, the nearest towns to the mining camp where Margaret's husband, Marcus, was the superintendent of the Zella Group of mines owned by the Walker Brothers syndicate. Marcus and Margaret had spoken their vows in the Salt Lake City home of Joseph Walker, one of the prominent banking and mining tycoons who had hired her husband. Marcus was convinced he could make the silver mines in Ophir very profitable.

Margaret believed he could, but she wasn't so sure about his story of the gypsy who had said great riches were coming to him. That could well be an Irishman's embroidery on his early days as an immigrant lad living on his wits in New York City. But he told the story well, with his rich brogue and twinkling eyes. He said that the gypsy had said she saw riches in his future—and if he wanted to know more he'd have to cross her palm with silver. Not having any silver to spare, he'd not heard the rest of the fortune-teller's tale.

A lot of silver had crossed his palms since that time, silver mined in Nevada and Utah. Perhaps the gypsy had been right. One thing eighteen-year-old Margaret knew for a fact was that her husband had been successful in the fifteen years since he'd departed from Ballyjamesduff, Ireland.

For Marcus, marrying the young woman who had literally fallen into his arms was the crowning success of his life so far. He had great expectations and huge ambitions for the future. Catching young Margaret Evans when she'd slipped going down an incline shaft was one of his luckiest accidents, and with his luck and nose for buried riches, he intended to prove to her that she'd married the right man.

Margaret's family included an Oxford-educated great grandfather and a Baptist minister grandfather. Marcus was the son of an Irish pig farmer, an immigrant with no more schooling than the little he'd received from his mother before he left for America at the age of fifteen.

Marcus Daly had arrived in New York City in 1856 and worked at whatever jobs he could find. His sister, Ann, lived in San Francisco, so he'd heard plenty of stories about the opportunities in California. By saving every dime he could, he scraped up enough by 1861 to set sail for the Golden State. After working at a number of odd jobs, he tried his hand at placer mining in Calaveras County.

He was too late to make a fortune in placer mining there, because the easy pickings had already been taken during the 1849 Gold Rush and the years that followed. By 1865 Marcus had headed west with a lot of other miners to the great Comstock silver boom in Nevada. While working in the silver mines, he learned more

DALY MANSION, HAMILTON, MT

Margaret Evans

about mining and made some important connections. His Irish luck had been strong the day he met George Hearst and J. B. Haggin, wealthy men trying to get richer in the Comstock silver boom. The men had become friends, and Hearst had given Marcus and Margaret silverware engraved with a fancy "D" for a wedding gift.

Marcus and Margaret arrived in Ophir not long after their

wedding. Ophir had little to commend it except the silver, Marcus thought. Margaret knew the mining town couldn't provide the culture and commerce of Salt Lake City, but with its almost-new city hall and firehouse, its general stores, drugstores, and post office, as well as the theaters, schools, and Chinese laundry, she felt confident that she could set up housekeeping in some degree of style. Plus, a stagecoach line run by Wines and Greathouse ran daily to Salt Lake City, so she could make the $5.00 trip when necessary.

Married life in a cottage near a silver mine brought challenges and triumphs for Margaret and her husband. Two daughters were born to the couple while they lived in Ophir, Margaret Augusta and Mary. Like other wives, Margaret packed her husband's lunch in a tin pail every day. She cleaned and cooked and even, according to some sources, took in laundry.

Meanwhile, Marcus was hard at work on and under Lion Hill. According to the April 18, 1874, edition of the *Salt Lake City Tribune*, "A number of veins of good ore have been struck. It is the intention of the company to run levels at each one hundred feet on these veins." At that time about one hundred tons of high-grade chloride ore was being removed daily from the four mines in the vicinity.

On April 15, 1874, Marcus Daly became a citizen of the United States. Perhaps he and Margaret celebrated the following week at a grand party in town. On April 28 the *Tribune* reported a "Magnificent Ball and Entertainment" was given at the beautiful hall built by the Ladies of Ophir. The occasion commemorated the fifty-fifth anniversary of the Odd Fellows. Sixty elegantly dressed local ladies reportedly attended, as well as people from Stockton, Tooele, and Lewiston.

By 1876 Marcus's talent for geology, his instincts for finding riches, and his experience and charm induced Walker Brothers to send Marcus to Montana Territory to look for more silver. He left

DALY MANSION, HAMILTON, MT

Marcus Daly

Margaret and his daughters in Ophir and headed to the straggling
town of Walkerville, at the top of the hill perched above Butte,
Montana. The Walkers instructed Marcus to buy mining properties
if he considered them of value. He purchased the Alice Mine, which
would soon be the vehicle that would fulfill the gypsy's prophecy,
keeping a small share for himself.

While wheeling and dealing for Walker Brothers, Marcus was pining for his family. In September 1877 he went back to Utah to retrieve his wife and children and settle them in Walkerville, where only a dozen or so small, gray houses were crowded around the mining sites.

Margaret did her best to create a home for her family in the cottage they rented on North Main Street. The stark extremes in temperatures, which varied from minus fifty degrees in winter to one hundred degrees in summer, were bad enough. Worse was the pollution created by the processing of ore. The steep hillsides were denuded of timber, which all had been used to create the underground workings of the mines or taken to the mills that turned raw ore into bullion by using a variety of toxic chemicals that were burned off in the final process. The lack of trees and tainted air made for a very unpleasant environment in Butte and the surrounding area.

In late 1877 Marcus began to sink a shaft at the Alice. The *Butte Miner* forecasted doom: "Mr. Daly is working eight-hour shifts, three men in a shaft. Water is coming in rapidly; it is about as much as the present facilities for hoisting can do to keep it down." Reporters were convinced the ore would disappear at the 500-foot level. It didn't, and the Alice went on to become one of the world's major producers of silver ore.

Marcus and Margaret were blessed not only with steadily increasing financial success. Two more children were born, Harriot (Hattie) Holes and a son, Marcus Daly, Jr. With four small children in tow, Marcus moved his family to a new home at Quartz and Montana Streets in Butte.

Then Marcus took a gamble. Although the Alice was reportedly averaging thirty to forty ounces of pure silver to the ton of ore, and from $4.00 to $12.00 in gold daily, Marcus sold the small share he owned in the mine for thirty thousand dollars, and then, very quietly, met with fellow Irishmen Edward and Daniel Hickey, two brothers who had a claim and a 65-foot-deep shaft they'd named the Anaconda.

Although the mine was little more than a hole in the ground at that point, Marcus noted the greenish color of some of the workings, suggesting that the soil was rich in copper. He tried to convince Walker Brothers to buy in, but they wanted nothing to do with it. Based on his years of experience in mining and on a hunch, Marcus offered to buy the claim for ten thousand dollars. According to the reminiscences of C. C. Goodwin of *Goodwin's Weekly*, ". . . [Marcus] said to me then that the world did not know it, but it would after a while, that he had the biggest mine ever found."

Marcus called on his old friend George Hearst, who, along with two other investors from San Francisco, provided enough financial backing for Marcus to buy up other played-out silver claims in the area. Some people say the prices on these claims dropped dramatically after rumors were circulated about problems with the claims; some say Marcus began the rumors while quietly buying up the devalued properties.

With virtually unlimited funds from his partners, Marcus Daly sank the original 65-foot Anaconda shaft 300 feet deeper—down past the silver ore—where he struck a large vein of copper ore approximately 100 feet wide. Marcus's Anaconda Company became the largest copper-mining company anywhere. By 1890 the Anaconda copper mine was producing more than seventeen million dollars' worth of copper a year. The Dalys became millionaires, and Margaret, a mining-camp bride, soon had a mansion on Fifth Avenue in New York City and a summer home in Montana's Bitterroot Valley.

In the pristine grasslands near the Bitterroot River, Marcus purchased some 22,000 acres of land. He laid out the town of

Hamilton with wide streets in a grid that made it easy to know exactly where you were. The Bitterroot Mountains rose abruptly to the west, and the Sapphires climbed more gently to the east. The toxic skies of Butte were far away, on the other side of the Sapphires. The 95-mile-long Bitterroot Valley was sheltered from the worst of the prevailing winds and was well watered by the river and many streams tumbling down from the forested mountainsides.

With the huge profits from the Anaconda, Marcus began buying up small ranches and farms in the Bitterroot Valley. At one time he had more than twenty thousand acres under cultivation, and with the addition of the ranch land he owned at Three Forks, his holdings totaled fifty thousand acres. Margaret and Marcus built a Victorian-style mansion they called Riverside on a portion of the land he'd purchased, and the Bitterroot Stock Farm was developed on prime lands in the valley east of Hamilton. There Marcus began to indulge a secret love for horses and racing.

A gambler at heart, Marcus began raising blooded horses and racing them. He maintained a stable in England and imported Irish and English horses. The *Liberty County Farmer* reported that Marcus kept in training, simultaneously, about fifty thoroughbreds and one hundred trotters and pacers. Marcus liked to win, but he also made good on his bets. In 1891 he bought a winning colt named Tammany, and two years later he vowed to build the horse a castle if it beat a rival racehorse named Lamplighter. Tammany beat Lamplighter by four lengths, and Marcus built the horse a brick stable complete with a Turkish bath. Tammany and other horses trained at the Dalys' stables and raced under colors of copper and green.

Marcus Daly was intensely involved in the Montana Capital Fight of 1894. Marcus wanted Anaconda to be the capital, whereas his political rival, William Andrews Clark, favored Helena. Helena won the honor after a bitter battle and a fraudulent election.

Through it all, Margaret stood by her husband's side.

Copper King and Queen Marcus and Margaret Daly began a complete overhaul of their mansion at the end of the nineteenth century. Drawings were made for a 21,000-square-foot residence with twenty-four bedrooms, fourteen bathrooms, seven fireplaces, and a state-of-the-art kitchen, in which Margaret took a particular interest. Landscaped grounds complete with swimming pool, tennis court, children's playhouse, greenhouse, and a number of other out-buildings eventually surrounded the three-story Georgian Revival–style mansion.

Marcus, however, did not live to see its completion. On November 12, 1900, the fifty-eight-year-old multimillionaire died in a room at the Netherlands Hotel in New York surrounded by his immediate family. A year later, in *Progressive Men of Montana*, the Irish immigrant who had proved a gypsy's prophecy, was eulogized.

> Marcus Daly was a remarkable man. The magnitude of his conceptions and his force of character cannot be overestimated. His sweep of vision was mighty and his will-power was tremendous. He threw himself into all his undertakings with a fixedness of purpose and a disregard for obstacles which compelled success.

According to one source Margaret was deeply depressed after her husband's death. Although he left some ten million dollars in cash as well as valuable investments, the money, the jewels, the huge ranch, and the social position she enjoyed could not make up for the loss of the strong Irishman who had caught her when she stumbled and held her close to his heart for all their years together.

Margaret Daly never remarried. She lived in Riverside for forty years after her husband's death.

Mary K. Cummings a.k.a. "Big Nose Kate"

The Outlaw Dentist and the Madam

He was close to six feet tall, weight—one hundred and sixty pounds, fair complexion, very pretty moustache, blue-gray eyes, and a fine set of teeth.
—KATE ELDER'S DESCRIPTION OF DOC HOLLIDAY, OCTOBER 1877

Kate Elder touched a lighted match to the back of the Griffith Hotel in Fort Griffith, Texas, and stood back to watch the building be overtaken by flames. She smiled to herself and then raced out into the street yelling, "Fire, fire!" Patrons hurried out of the hotel and joined the other citizens in a mad dash to the water barrels. While the town was preoccupied with putting out the blaze, Kate ran into the hotel and charged up the stairs.

A pair of bewildered guards stood outside a closed door fanning the smoke out of their faces. Kate pulled a six-shooter out of her drawstring purse and pointed it at the men. "Drop your guns and open the door or I'll shoot you down where you stand." The guards quickly tossed their weapons down, unlocked the door, and swung it open. She motioned for them to back off, and they reluctantly did as they were told.

A neatly groomed Doc Holliday stuck his head out of the room, looked around, and then sauntered over to Kate. "You are a wonder, darling," he told her. "They were going to hang me for ridding this earth of a snake who cheated at cards." Doc took the gun from Kate, and the two bounded down the stairs as the fire raged on. The pair leapt on the horses Kate had waiting for them and rode off into the night.

Kate would have done anything for John Henry "Doc" Holliday. She had loved him from the moment she saw him enter the saloon where she worked as a prostitute. He had an air of dignity and an anguished look in his eyes that drew her to him. He was taken with her as well. He despised "sporting girls" with blond hair, painted faces, and exposed legs. Kate better suited him. She was a quite young, tall, big-boned, brunette, and buxom woman with a nose so determined and handsome that she was called "Big Nose Kate."

He was also attracted to her fiery temper and fiercely independent nature. She had a true loving heart, a ready laugh, and a marvelous vocabulary of cuss words. Doc possessed the same qualities. Their combination made for a rocky relationship. They were two individuals seeking to shape their lives by their own rules.

Kate was born Mary Katherine Horony on November 17, 1850, in Budapest, Hungary. She came from an aristocratic family and was well educated, another element Doc found captivating. Kate came to the States with her family in 1865. Her parents died the following year, and Kate ran away from the foster home she was placed in and stowed away on a steamship headed for St. Louis. She changed her name and temporarily went to live in a convent. A failed marriage and the death of her infant son drove her west, where she hoped to forget the tragedies of her life.

Doc also came west to forget. John Henry Holliday was born to Alice Jane McKey and Henry Burroughs Holliday on August 14, 1851, in the tiny town of Griffin, Georgia. He attended the finest schools for the sons of Southern gentlemen. In his free time he roamed the woods around town, learning the ways of the wilderness.

John Henry "Doc" Holliday

He also took up pistol practice and was an excellent marksman by the time he was fourteen.

His life changed in 1866, when his mother died from the lung disease tuberculosis. She had been a stabilizing force in his life, and with her death came a melancholy that he would carry with him to his grave.

Relations between John and his father were strained when Henry married a twenty-year-old woman three months after his wife's funeral. John shot a Union soldier in an altercation over a watering hole shortly after the wedding. In an attempt to protect his son, John's father sent him to a dental college in Pennsylvania. Henry threw off bounty hunters looking for John by telling them his son was attending school in Baltimore.

John graduated in 1872 and returned home with a strange cough. He was diagnosed as having tuberculosis. Doctors told him that he wouldn't live six months in Georgia and suggested he move to Texas, where the climate was better. Just before he moved he attended the funeral of his brother, who had died of the same ailment. By the time Doc met up with Kate, he had made a name for himself as "the gambler dentist with the fast gun."

After Doc and Kate escaped from the burning Texas hotel, they headed for Dodge City, Kansas. Once there, Doc set up a dental practice, and the two moved into Deacon Cox's Boarding House, registered as "Mr. and Mrs. J. H. Holliday." Despite their registration as man and wife, there is no evidence that Kate and Doc ever legally married.

Doc played nightly card games with his new friends, Wyatt Earp and Bat Masterson. He began to spend less and less time with his dentistry practice, and late-night drinking brought on long bouts of sickness. Kate would stay by his side and help him get well. He loved her for it, but he also resented her good health. They fought constantly, and even though they lived as common-law husband and wife, Kate continued to work as a prostitute. Her job affected Doc's view of her, and he oftentimes treated her as inferior, but Kate didn't care enough to quit. She liked her occupation because it provided her with her own income and she didn't have to answer to anybody.

Doc needed Kate. She knew how to ease him through his coughing spells, and he actually enjoyed the volatile relationship they shared. He liked her coarseness and vulgarity. Wyatt Earp was witness to many of their fights and on several occasions suggested to Doc that he should "belt her one." Doc would reply, "Man cannot do what he wants to in this world, but only that which will benefit him."

It was no secret to Kate that Doc had once been madly in love with his first cousin, Mattie. Mattie was refined, petite, and soft-spoken, everything Kate wasn't. Doc would oftentimes fall into a depression over his lost love and lash out publicly at Kate for not being the lady he could have had.

One night after just such a show, Doc returned to the couple's hotel room to sleep off another night of drinking and forget the spectacle he had made of himself and Kate. A furious Kate followed him, banging loudly on the locked door. Doc was having a coughing fit and couldn't make it up off the bed to let her in. Kate busted down the door and bounded into the room with a big Colt gun in her hand. "You are a lousy son of a bitch!" she yelled. "I'm going to fill you so full of holes you won't float in brine!" Kate fired a shot into the mattress Doc was lying on. Doc jumped up, jerked the gun out of her hand, and cracked her over the head with it. Kate fell to the floor, bleeding. Doc stood over her, feeling sober and sorry. The two were not seen again until late the following afternoon, when they were holding hands and behaving like newlyweds.

The couple next moved to Trinidad, Colorado. Their stay was

cut short when Doc again fell ill. The pair relocated to the warmer climate in Las Vegas, New Mexico. Doc worked as a dentist during the day and ran a saloon at night. Kate plied her trade at a dance hall in nearby Santa Fe. The lovers made New Mexico their home for two years. They found Las Vegas to be a hospitable place, but many local citizens did not return the sentiment. An article in the *Las Vegas Optic*, published in July of 1881, two years after the pair had moved, explained how happy the townspeople were to see the two go.

> It will be remembered, especially by pioneers of the East Side, that Doc Holliday was at one time the keeper of a gin mill on Centre Street, near the site of the Centre Street Bakery. Doc was always considered a shiftless, bagged legged character—a killer and a professional cut-throat and not a wit too refined to rob stages or even steal sheep. . . . The woman, Elder . . . was a Santa Fe tid-bit and surrounded her habiliments with a detestable odor before leaving the "Ancient" [City] that will in itself make her memory immortal.

In 1879 Wyatt Earp rode into town on his way to Arizona and convinced Doc to go along with him. Kate was not happy with their plans and wrote about her desires in a letter to her niece in March of 1940.

> I wanted Doc to stay with me. I told Doc that, but Wyatt told him that Arizona was the better place to be. Wyatt had his wife and brother James and his wife and daughter with him. We arrived in Prescott in November. Doc and I went to the hotel. Virgil Earp, the oldest brother, was already in Prescott. Was there two years ahead of us.

Doc followed the poker games in Prescott, and Kate followed Doc. The Earps went on to Tombstone, but Doc had hit a lucky streak and decided to stay in Prescott until it played out. Kate wanted to move to Globe, Arizona. She had heard the miners there had lots of money to spend and saw it as an opportunity for her and Doc to make a fortune. Kate pleaded with Doc not to go to Tombstone, but his mind was made up to go after his luck ran out in Prescott. Kate complained to her niece that "the Earps had such a power I could not get Doc away from them."

Doc joined the Earps in Tombstone in 1880, without Kate.

Kate moved to Globe and bought herself a hotel with the money she had made in Santa Fe. Doc, meanwhile, still in Tombstone, continued drinking heavily and gambling until dawn. It wasn't long before he began writing letters to Kate, begging her to visit him. "I missed Doc terribly and so I went to see him," Kate told her niece. "I had to pay a friend to look after my interest in the hotel, but off I went like a moth to a flame."

Kate arrived in Tombstone in March of 1881. By that time Doc was very thin and pale. His bright eyes were fading to a cold, hard gray, and his head was topped by enough white hairs to make his hair appear ash blond. His tuberculosis had become a habit; he couldn't remember what it was like to feel good. Alcoholism was continuing to deteriorate his personality, and his hangovers were marvels to behold. He had a foul disposition and could only work up the energy to be kind to his close friends. He was angry over his frequent impotency and took it out on Kate through public outbursts. Then one day a broken heart and bottle of cheap whiskey drove her to retaliate.

On the night of March 15, 1881, armed robbers attempted to hold up a stage near the town of Contention, Arizona. In the holdup attempt the robbers killed the driver and a passenger. A drunken Kate later told Cochise County Sheriff Behan and his deputy, Frank Stillwell, that Doc was responsible for the robbery and murders, and she signed an affidavit to the fact. Doc was arrested and thrown in jail.

When Kate was sober and realized what she had done, she repudiated the statement, and the judge dropped the charges. An angry Doc gave Kate some money and a stagecoach ticket and sent her back to Globe.

In October Kate received another letter from Doc asking her to return to Tombstone. Kate hurried back and moved into Doc's room at Fly's Boarding House, where the two were happy for a short time. Doc took her to a fiesta in Tucson. During their time there Morgan Earp found them and told Doc he would be needed in Tombstone the next day. Doc told Kate to stay behind in Tucson, but strong-willed Kate insisted she would go back to Tombstone with him.

They arrived back in town, and that night Kate and Doc settled into their room overlooking the OK Corral. The next morning Kate awoke before Doc and soon heard the news that Ike Clanton, a member of a cattle-rustling gang of outlaws who was feuding with the Earps and their friends, was looking for Doc Holliday. When she told Doc the news, he replied, "If God will let me live to get my clothes on, he shall see me." Kate later recalled, "With that he got up, dressed, and went out. As he went out, he said, 'I may not be back to take you to breakfast, so you better go alone.' I didn't go to breakfast. I don't remember eating anything that day."

It wasn't long before Kate heard shooting nearby and went to a side window. From there, she and a Mrs. C. S. Fly watched the fight. She wrote her eyewitness account of the events in her journal.

Almost at the same time I saw Virgil Earp, Wyatt, Morgan Earp and Doc Holliday coming to the vacant lot from

Fremont Street. They stood ten feet apart when the shooting began. Ike Clanton ran and left his younger brother Billy. I saw Doc fall but he was up as quick as he fell. Something went wrong with his rifle, he threw his rifle on the ground and pulled out his six-shooter. Every shot he fired got a man. Billy Clanton was killed as were the two McLaurys. Virgil and Morgan Earp got shot as well. It is foolish to think that a cow rustler gun man can come up to a city gun man in a gunfight.

During the fight a bullet broke two windowpanes above Kate, but she never stopped watching. Fortunately, Doc suffered only a minor grazing on the back. The gunfight, however, landed Doc and Wyatt Earp in jail for a time, and although a judge acquitted Doc and the Earps of murder, Kate returned to Globe for safety.

Following the gunfight Kate remained in Globe for several years. In 1887 she received word of Doc being near death, and she traveled to Colorado to be with him. Historical records indicate that she took him to her brother Alexander's ranch near Glenwood Springs. Doc died in a Glenwood Springs hotel on November 8, 1887.

In 1888 Kate married George Cummings, a blacksmith. Their marriage was troubled from the beginning. It seems Cummings lacked the passion and ability to spar with her that Doc had. Kate eventually left George; he later committed suicide.

Kate lived out the rest of her life in Arizona. Several ambitious reporters tried to persuade her to let them pen a book about her life and relationship with Doc Holliday. She declined all invitations to do so because no one wanted to pay her for her tale.

Kate moved into the Arizona Pioneer's Home in 1935. She passed away five years later on November 2. Letters Kate wrote her niece show that she carried a torch for her tormented Doc Holliday to the very end.

Mollie Walsh

The Packer and the Klondike Angel

JACK NEWMAN AND MOLLIE WALSH

> *I'm a better man, a better citizen, for having known Mollie Walsh. She influenced me always for the good. Her spirit fingers still reach across the years and play on the slackened strings of my old heart, and my heart still sings, Mollie! My heart still sings but in such sad undertone that none but God and I can hear.*
>
> —JACK NEWMAN, 1930

Mollie Walsh raced out of her house on Pike Street, in Seattle, crying. A look of panic filled her face. It was October 27, 1902. It was raining. Mollie was petrified and sick with the flu. She glanced over her shoulder just in time to see her husband, Michael Bartlett, burst through the front door and come after her. He swore at her and shouted for her to stop, but she only ran faster. Mike Bartlett pulled a revolver out of his pocket, took aim, and fired two shots. Both bullets hit Mollie in the back. She fell face first into the mud, reeled up once, and then died. She was thirty years old.

Not long after, Jack Newman, a handsome man with a square jaw and lively chestnut hair, sat at the bar at Clancy's Saloon in Skagway, Alaska. A few tears fell into his beer. With his big fist he wiped the other tears he couldn't hold back off his face and mustache. In his hand he held a dog-eared photograph of Mollie Walsh and a copy of her obituary he had found in the *Klondike Nugget* newspaper. "To have known such a great and exalted love," Jack mumbled to himself, "and have it flee from your grasp." Jack took his drink over to the window to watch a heavy snow blanket the soggy streets and remember his great and exalted love.

Mollie Walsh was lured to Alaska in 1897. Gold had just been discovered in the Klondike, and like other "stampeders," Mollie embarked on a journey for fortune and glory. She was a diminutive and gracious woman of twenty-six with long, dark hair and a dusting of freckles across her nose. She arrived in Skagway in October and worked as a cook and waitress in one of the town's nineteen restaurants. She saved her money and eventually opened her own "tent road house" near the tiny mining town of Log Cabin.

Mollie's Grub Tent was a popular establishment. She provided good food and supplies for gold miners and packers hiking through the cold, snowy mountains. She faithfully attended church services held under a lean-to. When it came time for a church building to be constructed, Mollie helped raise the funds for Log Cabin's first Union Church. Reverend Dickey, the pastor of the church, was impressed with Mollie's eagerness to lend a hand whenever needed and with her delightful disposition. He was highly complimentary of her sense of humor as well. In December of 1897 he wrote in his journal that "Miss Walsh was a pretty, Irish girl, full of fun and not averse to making fun of herself in a crowd. When teased about being 'an old Maid,' she admitted to having had three proposals, back home in Montana."

No one was more taken by Mollie's fine character than Jack Newman. Mollie first caught Jack's attention when she risked her reputation and the censure of the respectable women of the area to nurse a sick girl at a brothel. When the woman died, Mollie asked Reverend Dickey to hold her funeral at the church.

Packer Jack Newman (center) near Skagway, Alaska, 1898

In his eulogy the reverend urged the prostitutes in attendance to quit their profession. Captain Samuel O'Brien of the S.S. *Shamrock* attended the funeral and was so moved by the sermon that he offered free passage to Seattle for any woman who wanted to leave Alaska. Mollie raised money to give to the women so that they could make a fresh start. Many left on the S.S. *Shamrock* that night.

Mollie was well known for her generosity to all. Jack was the recipient of her kindness on more than one occasion. One night while Jack was packing his way through the mountains, he got caught in a bitter snowstorm. Almost blinded, his left hand frozen, he stumbled into Mollie's trailside tent. Mollie helped Jack to a table, served him hot coffee, and rubbed his hand until the circulation returned. Jack recalled that tender moment in his memoirs, written in 1902: "A strange feeling passed between us as Mollie tended to my frost-bitten hand. I left her tent with a great love flooding my heart."

"Packer Jack" Newman had rarely seen the benevolence Mollie practiced. Being a roughneck mountain man, he primarily kept company with those just like him. According to his friends Jack was a complex fellow. He was a philosopher, altruist, poet, and two-handed pistol shot champion. He had fought Indians and driven pack trains in the early days of Arizona, Colorado, and Alaska. He was a determined man and a success at whatever he set out to do.

Jack set his sights on Mollie. Every chance he got he would stop into her grub tent and visit with her. But Jack wasn't the only suitor vying for her attention. A faro dealer had his eye on Mollie as well. Word got back to Jack that the gambler had called him a "low-down shaggy wolf." Jack called the dealer out into the street to settle things once and for all. A large crowd looked on as Jack and the faro dealer drew on each other. Jack beat the gambler to the draw and shot him in the leg. "I promised you I wouldn't kill him," Jack told Mollie, "but I had to make it hard for him to keep running to your place anymore."

The more time Jack spent with Mollie, the more in love with her he fell. Mollie cared a great deal for Jack, but she wasn't convinced they were a match. She eventually wanted to move to a more populated, congenial spot. Jack preferred frontier living, miles away from the grind of city life.

Mollie's Grub Tent was an oasis in the desert for many packers. They looked forward to getting a good meal at her establishment and chatting with the friendly, gracious woman. Thirty-two-year-old Michael Bartlett happened into her business establishment one afternoon. He was tall, handsome, and hardworking. His family had come to Alaska from Texas and quickly became wealthy selling supplies, livestock, and machinery to the miners. Mike was instantly smitten with Mollie and began spending a lot of time at her restaurant. Jack didn't like Mike Bartlett paying so much attention to

Mollie and let it be known. Mike replied that "rights claimed by Newman in business or love were of no concern to him." Jack ordered Mollie not to let Mike into her tent. His demands did not set well with her. Jack later said of that day: "Mollie was angry, for sure. She said I wasn't her master, not being married to her, and this was a public eating place, so anyone in the whole northland was welcome. One thing led to another. Trifle piled on trifle. Neither of us would weaken."

Mollie grew tired of the filth and corruption that ran rampant in the little mining town and began making plans to relocate. Jack wanted her to stay but knew he couldn't make her happy living in a place she didn't want to be, and he didn't want to leave his profitable business as a packer. In June of 1898 Mollie moved to Dawson. In December she married Mike Bartlett. Packer Jack's heart was broken.

The Bartletts were happy for a time. Mike moved Mollie into a beautiful, vine-covered cottage. She eagerly accepted the domestic responsibilities and social obligations befitting the wife of a successful businessman. Problems began early on for the couple, however. Mollie was not well liked by Mike's family. His brothers had opposed the marriage. They believed Mollie had married Mike for his money and felt she had a questionable past. They didn't believe Mollie merely ran a grub tent for packers. They accused her of being a prostitute. Mollie's spirit of enterprise further added to her in-law dilemma. When she decided to take a break from her domestic life and become involved with the family business, her in-laws did not approve. To escape the turmoil Mike moved Mollie to Seattle. Shortly thereafter he traveled back to Alaska to take care of the Bartlett brothers' interests in Nome.

Jack's gold-miner friends traveling back and forth from Seattle to Skagway kept tabs on Mollie and would let the broken-hearted

Jack know how she was doing. He tried his best to forget her and buried himself in his work, but she never left his mind for long. In 1900, when he heard she had given birth to a son, he thought about her, and when he got word that her husband's business was failing and he was gambling and drinking, he thought about her even more.

Rumor had it that Mike was abusing Mollie, and Jack ached for her. He was encouraged when news came that she had left Mike Bartlett and was headed for Skagway. He hoped he could catch up with her and they could get back together, but Mike had other plans for Mollie. He was frantic to find her and his son. He chased them all over the country—even to Mexico. When he finally found his family, he promised Mollie he would change and begged her to return to Seattle with him. Mollie agreed. Jack was devastated.

The Barletts' reconciliation was short-lived. Mike's behavior did not improve, and Mollie left him again. She withdrew a substantial amount of money from their bank account and moved into a boardinghouse. Mike found out where she was living and paid her a visit. He asked her to come home with him, and when she wouldn't, he tried to kill himself with a pistol. The shot, which lodged in the ceiling, attracted police officers, but Mollie told them that "he was not crazy and would hurt no one but himself." At her request he was not prosecuted.

The pair decided to separate and come to an understanding regarding finances. Mike drank more and more. Mollie felt sorry for him and proposed that they reunite. Mike readily accepted her offer, but soon Mike's violent temper overtook him again. This time Mollie had him arrested. She told the officers that her husband "abused her in all ways which he could devise, called her all the names nature could suggest, and had often threatened to make away with her existence."

A judge found Mike guilty of threatening to kill his wife and

ALONE WITHOUT HELP
THIS COURAGEOUS GIRL
RAN A GRUB TENT
NEAR LOG CABIN
DURING THE GOLD RUSH
OF 1897-1898
SHE FED AND LODGED
THE WILDEST
GOLD CRAZED MEN
GENERATIONS
SHALL SURELY KNOW
THIS INSPIRING SPIRIT
MURDERED OCT 27
1902

*Jack Newman's tribute to Mollie today stands in
Mollie Walsh Park, Skagway, Alaska.*

sentenced him to thirty days in jail. Mollie persuaded the judge to suspend her husband's sentence, because she was afraid that if he were placed in jail he would kill her as soon as his time was up. The judge reluctantly agreed to Mollie's request. Mike assured the court he "would not harm a hair on his wife's head." One week after his release, Michael Bartlett shot and killed Mollie in a fit of jealous anger.

Jack followed Mike's trial closely, as did all of Seattle. The court case dragged on for more than a year. Mike claimed Mollie's unfaithfulness had driven him to take her life. He was acquitted of the murder charge by reason of insanity; the court said he had committed a "crime of passion." Two years after the trial Mike Bartlett committed himself to an asylum and later committed suicide.

Packer Jack married in 1906, but he never got over his love for the woman he referred to as the "Angel of the Klondike Trail." In 1930 he had a bronze statue of Mollie made and sent it to Skagway. At present, her likeness stands at the entrance of Mollie Walsh Park. Jack wrote the inscription etched in granite beneath the bust: ALONE WITHOUT HELP—THIS COURAGEOUS GIRL RAN A GRUB TENT NEAR LOG CABIN DURING THE GOLD RUSH OF 1897–1898. SHE FED AND LODGED THE WILDEST GOLD CRAZED MEN GENERATIONS SHALL SURELY KNOW. THIS INSPIRING SPIRIT WAS MURDERED ON OCTOBER 27, 1902.

Before Jack died he asked his wife of twenty-four years to bury him on the White Pass Trail, where he believed the spirit of Mollie still lived.

The Tycoon's Heir and the Actress

TOM NOYES AND BELLE FRANCES ALLEN

She has always been respected by all who came to know her and probably was the most known person in Alaska by the old timers who knew she did things while they thought about doing them.

—WILLIAM MUNCASTER'S DESCRIPTION OF BELLE FRANCES ALLEN, 1952

*I*shall conduct no training school for actresses," Montana mining tycoon John Noyes declared. He sent his son Tom a withering glare. The boy had obviously been taken in by a pretty face. Mrs. Allen was not the type of woman he had in mind as a wife for his son. She'd been married and divorced, and that scandal had hardly quieted when a new one had erupted.

The full weight of his father's displeasure only strengthened Tom's resolve. "You have $2,500 in a trust fund that you are holding for me, have you not, Father?"

"Yes."

"Well, give me that. I will start out for myself, and you can cut me off without a cent." Tom had loved Belle Frances Allen ever since he first saw her in a theatrical production. His father thought Tom was too young to marry and Frances too infamous to be his bride, but Tom intended to marry her, and soon. Frances clearly was in danger, however, as another would-be suitor from New Orleans was stalking her from state to state and might soon appear in Butte.

Tom did not change his mind, though his father continually

dredged up the infamy of Frances's past, starting with her divorce from Samuel Allen earlier in 1897. The newspapers had reported every titillating development. According to one account Samuel Allen had told his friends that his ex-wife "is a good woman, but has a passion for money, a siren who uses her charms to infatuate men to the point where they lavish their wealth upon her, but she never strays from the straight and narrow path."

A report in Spokane's *Spokesman* entitled "She's An Actress, Ex-Prosecuting Attorney Objects to that Life" claimed, "The wreck of this family commenced about the time of the society circus at Natatorium Park in 1895, when Mrs. Allen rode two horses bareback. Mr. Allen did not enjoy this exhibition, and the family was never a happy one."

Tom suspected his father had seen that article. He was certain the electrifying accounts had convinced his father to forbid him to marry the woman he loved. The newspapers, in Tom's opinion, wrongly made Frances sound like a beautiful but heartless, money-hungry tease. Tom's father certainly believed this and reminded his son that no respectable woman would flaunt herself on the stage unless she was out to snare a rich husband. Tom knew Frances did not care about money. She would marry him with his small trust fund and no prospects of inheriting his father's huge fortune.

What worried Tom was the threat hanging over Frances's life. A would-be suitor, Alfred Hildreth, was stalking Frances, and his actions had steadily become more dangerous. At the Leland Hotel in Chicago, Hildreth had lain in wait for five days. The Southerner confronted Frances in the lobby, and witnesses said Frances agreed to dine with him at a downtown restaurant, only to have the impassioned swain brandish a carving knife while declaring he would do something desperate if she wouldn't have him. He had followed Frances through several states, and his ardor increased every time he

Frances and Tom Noyes

caught up with her. Tom knew Alfred could show up at any time.

Newspapers in Chicago and New York recorded the tales of Hildreth's obsession. The *Chicago Chronicle* carried one story that made Tom's blood boil.

Alfred J. Hildreth loves Mrs. Frances Allen with such true and ardent affection that he has followed her 5,000 miles to prove it. Even though Mr. Allen secured a divorce from his wife because she rode bareback at a charity circus in Spokane, Wash., attired in the reddest of red silken tights, Hildreth says she is dear to him. Mrs. Allen, however, does not return the feeling of young Hildreth, and she has spent many weary hours moving from one city to another to escape the devoted lover.

The tights had been pink, but Tom didn't bother to correct the story. Frances Allen belonged to him, and neither Alfred Hildreth nor Tom's own father was going to stand in the way of a wedding, Tom decided.

Arabella Frances Patchen Allen did not care that Tom's father disapproved of her life on the stage. She intended to marry his son. Of all the men who had pursued her since she had left Spokane after the fateful circus ride, Tommy was the one she truly loved. Her first marriage had been troubled from the start. On the day of her wedding to Samuel Allen in 1892, when she was barely eighteen, the groom had disappeared. His drunken companions had held a "special session" and voted to continue the wedding anyway, with a different groom. After several good-natured votes were taken among the unmarried men, each of whom had voted for himself, Samuel had finally reappeared, and the vows were spoken.

For a few years she had enjoyed the social life that was part of being married to a prominent lawyer. Samuel had even given his consent for her participation in the charity circus at Natatorium Park, since half the money would go to the family of a boy who had broken his back in a barrel slide. Her husband had stalked out in a rage when he discovered his beautiful young wife in form-fitting tights and short blue skirt, riveting the attention of every person in the place.

Samuel's outrage had resulted in a huge quarrel, and she'd left his fine home for good that August. By April of the following year, she had succeeded on the stage. If she hadn't ridden in the society circus, she might still be married to Samuel and living well, she knew, but by leaving Spokane and taking parts in productions in Bradford, Pennsylvania, she'd achieved some success of her own. And her acting career had allowed her to meet Tom Noyes, whom she had fallen in love with and was prepared to marry.

The 1897 wedding of Tom Noyes and Belle Frances Allen did not compare in any way to Tom's sister's wedding, which linked two prosperous mining families and was celebrated as the most brilliant wedding ever held in Montana. Tom and Belle were married in a small, quiet ceremony. By the time Tom's sister, Ruth Noyes, married Arthur Heinz, Tom and Belle were already mining together in Skagway, Alaska, at the foot of a glacier on Otter Creek.

Tom knew he was a lucky man. Not many women would have smiled through the bitter cold and long darkness of an Alaskan winter. Unlike the California Gold Rush, few women had hurried to the rush in the frozen northland. But his petite, flirtatious Frances was one of a handful of women truly interested in mining. She loved the open country and the freedom from the society that had scorned her.

Frances was as eager as Tom to move on when Otter Creek didn't provide the wealth they were seeking. They headed for wide-open, lawless Nome, located at the edge of the Seward Peninsula on the Bering Sea. Gold had been discovered at Anvil Creek, and by the spring of 1900, somewhere between twenty and thirty thousand "stampeders" had come to Nome.

Camped above the tide line with thousands of others, Frances, who stood approximately 2 inches shorter than 5 feet tall, helped shovel sand into the portable rockers used to sift out the fine gold. Many people believed that the ocean was depositing gold at high tide. Tents and rockers stretched for miles along the beach.

Tom was appointed to a four-year term as a U.S. Commissioner for the Fairhaven District of Alaska, and soon Frances and Tom were again moving in the upper circles of society, albeit a much more flamboyant elite than the stuffy and conventional social strata they'd left behind. Tom's knowledge of mining and his impeccable character, dubbed "pure gold" by one of the men he worked with on several claims, earned respect in lawless Nome.

Tom wanted to find the Alaska mother lode, and Frances was always ready to follow where he led. He learned from one of the native people in the area that gold was easier to get on Candle Creek. Frances put away her silks and lace and followed Tom hundreds of miles north to Candle Creek, where they staked several claims. Frances experienced "mushing" by dogsled and began to learn more and more about prospecting.

Alaskan newspapers covered some of the adventures of the prospecting newlyweds, reporting that they endured "perilous trips, lost trails, climbs over glacial fields, where steps had to be cut with an ax." More than once Frances was credited with saving her husband's life. Their claims paid off, and Tom became known as "King of the Candle." He started a bank and built a home for himself and Frances, where anyone was welcome.

In 1902 Tom's father died, and Tom inherited an interest in a hotel in Seattle. Success piled on success, and Frances and Tom began to alternate between harsh conditions and adventures in Alaska and society teas and balls in Seattle and Butte.

In 1905 Tom and Frances adopted a half-Eskimo girl, Bonnie who was approximately five years old. During the winter she attended school in Butte; in the summer she often returned to Alaska with her parents.

As their success at Candle grew, Tom conceived of a plan to

Mining claim at Candle Creek, circa 1910.
Tom and Frances Noyes are seated in the center.

bring water to the rich placer diggings. In the autumn of 1907, he left for New York to obtain $200,000 to finance the completion of the Bear Creek ditch. Frances stayed at Candle to manage their interests.

He'd barely arrived in New York when a financial panic hit, jeopardizing the nation's economy. No bank would loan him money for a project in Alaska, and funds were so tight Tom had to pawn his watch and jewelry to pay his hotel bills. Tom's bank in Candle and the bank in Nome were threatened with a run by frightened customers eager to get their money into their own hands.

In an unprecedented feat of courage and strength, Frances once again came to her husband's rescue, only this time she saved his financial life. Pawning her jewelry to raise ten thousand dollars,

Frances mushed across the frozen Arctic tundra in the dead of winter. The story was printed in the *Seattle Times* and many other newspapers.

> With only a driver for her team of malamutes, she started out across the hundreds of miles of ice and snow, the thermometer so low it almost faded from view.
>
> Through the short days and into the nights this brave woman trudged on through the snow. Many days were needed for the journey, but the news that the money was coming had spread a better feeling in Nome and the bank was able to weather the storm until relief should arrive. The journey made by Mrs. Noyes was one of the most heroic ever attempted by a woman on her own initiative in the far North, and when she reached Nome she was accorded a welcome that was commensurate with her feat. The bank was saved, and a woman had been the agent.

Unfortunately, two years later Tom's bank failed, and his claims at Candle were lost. Tom had made a critical mistake—failing to use his official bank title when he signed checks—that left him personally liable when the bank failed. Tom and Frances retreated to Tongass Island near Ketchikan. In 1913 Tom ventured out to try his luck during a stampede to the Shushana gold strike. Shortly afterward, Frances joined him. There the harsh conditions of the Alaskan goldfields took their final toll.

Although they met with some success, one of the prospecting trips they took resulted in disaster. Days on the trail in temperatures as low as fifty degrees below zero with little shelter and poor food left Tom a "physical wreck."

On December 15, 1915, Tom was hospitalized in Port Simpson

General Hospital in British Columbia. Frances slept on a cot in his room, watching over and caring for him. Later, with Frances and his mother at his side, he was taken to a hospital in St. Louis, but he died of pneumonia on February 2, 1916.

Stunned and heartbroken, their fortune gone, Frances returned alone to Tongass Island. She received a letter that spring from one of their former partners who recalled Tom and Frances's early days at Otter Creek.

> Nearly 17 years ago you said goodbye to me on the platform at Seattle and you knew that you were saying farewell to a friend who would have done anything for you. I have not altered. I am just the same William you knew at Otter Creek and in our little camp at the foot of the glacier.

The letter goes on to remember Tom.

> I shall never realize that Tommy is dead. Since I left you I have been in many places and had dealings with many men, but I have never come across another Tommy, he was just pure gold. I was trying to think last night if I could remember him being out of temper or cross, but I could not, and we had some trying times. It is a great thing to have had a partner in life who you can look forward to meeting, to whom you can hold your hand out to and look straight in the eye and say "Tommy, I am glad to see you."
>
> Perhaps there may be another Klondike for us beyond the clouds; if there is I could ask for nothing better than my two dear friends of the glacier should be my partners again.

The writer advised Frances not to return to Alaska, but the

woman who had married at eighteen, divorced at twenty-three, and married again that same year to a man she cherished despite the scorn and anger of her father-in-law, returned to the northern land she loved. She kept body and soul together by managing the Nakat Inlet cannery store, but her love of the Alaskan wilderness eventually lured her away from civilization. She went back to prospecting, where everything she'd learned from her beloved Tommy allowed her to prosper.

Frances Noyes married again at the age of forty-five, to William Muncaster, who was 15 years younger. Despite the age difference, Bill had been smitten for years with the still-beautiful Frances. He'd sent her love letters and stopped in to visit her between trips to survey Alaska for the Coast and Geodetic Survey. Bonnie accompanied Frances and her new stepfather on their honeymoon trip to Alaska's goldfields.

Frances and William lived in a cabin on Wellesley Lake. They prospected and often went on fishing and hunting trips even when the temperature dipped to fifty below zero. Tom's memory, however, never faded for Frances. Visiting a place she and Tom had stayed during the Shushana gold strike, she wrote in her diary, "Everything looks different. Everything is different."

One thing that never changed was Frances's love of prospecting. She and William visited their claims until 1946, when Frances was seventy-two years old and living in Haines, a small town in southeastern Alaska.

The woman who scandalized Spokane with her daring ride in pink tights, the actress who caused a mining tycoon to shun his heir, the woman who saved her husband's bank with a grueling trek across the frozen northland, the unlikely prospector who loved Alaska so much she spent fifty-four years there, died on October 28, 1952. William Muncaster provided the press with clippings and stories about her life in Alaska. He wrote a final letter for the local newspaper.

Dear Sir,

Please publish this letter, for I wish to thank with all my heart all the people, young and old alike, in the town of Haines, Alaska, and the adjoining vicinities North, South, East and West for the unbelievable 100 percent respect shown by them at Mrs. Frances Muncaster's final rites. I thank you.

William Muncaster

Jim Averill

The Rancher and His Paramour

The lynching of Postmaster Averill and his wife on the Sweetwater Sunday night occurred about as reported in this paper yesterday morning. A Carbon County deputy Sheriff has laid himself liable to trouble by invading Fremont County with an armed posse and threatening to arrest the lynchers.

—CHEYENNE DAILY LEADER, JULY 24, 1889

As Ella "Kate" Watson sashayed down the crude staircase of the Rawlins saloon and brothel where she worked, she inspected the potential customers in the smoke-filled bar. Eager cowboys eyed her hourglass form as she brushed by them. They sniffed the air after her, breathing in the scent of jasmine she left behind. Kate looked past the scruffy wranglers vying for her attention and fixed her gaze on a tall, lean, well-dressed man sitting alone at a table, drinking.

"I'm Kate," she purred to the handsome gentlemen as she walked up to him. "Would you like some company?"

The man nodded, smoothed down his mustache, and slammed down another shot of whiskey. "Jim Averill. Pleased to meet you."

Kate had seen Jim Averill in the saloon before. He wasn't like any of the other men who frequented the Wyoming bordellos she'd worked in. He had an air of sophistication about him. Jim was a civil engineer and a gifted writer who had served in the army. His entrepreneurial spirit had driven him west to make his fortune in whatever venture presented itself. When Kate and Jim met in December of 1887, Jim was ranching. He owned a small spread along the Sweetwater River where the Rawlins-Lander stageline crossed the Oregon Trail. The supply store he had opened up at the stage stop was very profitable. He sold groceries, whiskey, and other items cowboys fancied they needed.

Kate had long since given up hope of ever meeting an accomplished man like Jim Averill. She was the daughter of a wealthy farmer in Smith County, Kansas, and was accustomed to fine things. In her teens she married a man who promised to provide her with the lifestyle she was raised in, but the marriage ended when she found him with another woman.

By the time she was twenty, Kate was divorced and earning a living as a prostitute in Wyoming. She preferred to work at houses in cow towns rather than bergs near army outposts. Cowboys paid better.

Kate was too ambitious to remain a common percentage girl. She was always looking for new opportunities—opportunities that would lead her to a position of wealth and power. Jim Averill possessed the same drive, and Kate fell in love with him. After the two enjoyed a few days of pleasure, Jim rode back to his ranch. Kate was left alone in her crib, praying that he would return her feelings. But Jim Averill had other things on his mind for the time being.

The years between 1887 and 1892 were a time of tension between big ranchers and small operators like Jim. Larger ranchers used vast areas of government land for grazing their cattle, yet they actually owned only a small parcel of land on which to build their homes. Small ranchers could use only land that they actually owned to graze their cattle. The power in Wyoming counties naturally rested with the big ranchers who operated the Wyoming Stock Grower's Association and who had substantial backing in the territorial legislature.

"Cattle Kate" Watson

Successful Jim Averill was a thorn in the association's side, and he made their secret "hit" list after refusing to vacate his property and give up his land. He further fueled the rift when he agreed to become the spokesperson for the smaller ranching operations.

Jim brought the small rancher's case into the public eye by writing numerous letters to the editors of Casper newspapers. He also used other tactics, such as forcing his opponents to prove their claim to the lands on which their ranches were located.

Kate had heard about the war between large ranch owners and small homesteaders. Not a night went by that there wasn't a saloon fight over who had rights to various pieces of land. Kate's business decreased as the trouble escalated. Her clients were preoccupied with the range war.

Kate was staring out her window, drinking in the sun, when the barkeep handed her a letter from Jim. A broad smile filled her face as she carefully opened the neatly penned, purple-prose letter. "My dearest Kate, I need you here with me. Please say you'll come. Always, Jim."

Kate was thrilled. This was proof that Jim Averill loved her. She set her sights on the two of them getting married and amassing a cattle fortune. She quickly sent word back to Jim that she was on her way.

When she arrived at his ranch, Jim helped Kate off her horse and kissed her. The two held each other for a moment; then Kate pulled away from her lover in order to have a look around. Jim's cabin and general store were rustic, but they were set against the backdrop of pretty rolling hills and a sparkling river. The range that spread out before them was dotted with cattle. Jim had a good start on a herd, and Kate was awash with enthusiasm imagining the possibilities for their future.

Jim had his sights set on the future as well. His position as spokesperson for the small ranchers served as the perfect entree into politics. He had become postmaster and justice of the peace for his district, and he believed these new positions would bring him credibility with the territorial legislature. He could state his case for homesteaders and force the government to enact laws to protect the landowners in Sweetwater Valley.

Jim wanted one of those landowners to be Kate. Any idea she had about setting up house with the man she loved was quickly extinguished. Jim moved Kate onto her own ranch—a piece of land Jim had filed for under the Homesteader's Act, using Kate's name.

It didn't take long for Jim to convince Kate that two homesteads meant the chance for financial security. According to the Homestead Act, the two merely had to live on the land for five years, and it would then belong to them. Jim promised to marry Kate when they had made final proof on their homesteads. Kate agreed and moved her things into the ranch house Jim had built for her, a log structure with a pale green door and shutters to match.

Kate proved to be a drawing card at Jim's store. Men would come from miles around just to look at her. Women were revered in Wyoming. The *Wyoming State Journal* reported that, in Wyoming, there was one woman for every one hundred men. Jim installed a bar in the back of his establishment, and it was frequented by cowhands from every big and small ranch in the valley.

Jim considered Kate to be a good investment. Kate was eager to please her betrothed, not only because she loved Jim, but because she loved money and everything that went along with it.

Jim and his men rounded up range strays, branded them with Jim's own brand, and shipped them off to eastern markets. Kate and Jim quickly became two of the richest ranchers in the area. Jim bought expensive clothes, gold cufflinks, and watch chains, and he even sent off for imported cigars. He took Kate on shopping trips to Denver, where she bought new dresses by the dozen.

All the while Jim kept up his barrage against the Stock Grower's Association. Members of the association, upset with Jim's ever-increasing wealth, continued to issue warnings to him to vacate his property or be killed. Jim refused to be scared off.

Jim was so preoccupied with planning the demise of the Wyoming Stock Grower's Association that he started to ignore Kate. In retaliation Kate kept company with some of the cowboys who came into the store. She would accept stolen cattle from the men in return for her favors, thus earning her the nickname "Cattle Kate."

Stories soon spread that stolen yearlings could be found among Kate's cattle. If they could not be seen in her pasture, it was alleged, it was because she was passing them on to Jim. The Stock Grower's Association accused Jim of being the head of a gigantic rustling ring. No evidence was produced that Jim was a rustler, but the association was intent on blackening his reputation and driving him out of the valley.

Jim was quick to come to his fiancée's defense. He loved her and didn't believe the rumors he felt were perpetrated by the association. He chose instead to believe that Kate had bought the yearlings outright with money he had given her.

In early July of 1889, an article championing both Jim and Kate's actions appeared in the newspaper *Bill Barlow's Budget*. Jim's hired hands later told historians that he was humiliated by the piece. It read: "Averill is not a rustler, and while his woman, Watson, did have stolen stock in her possession it is a fact that she, herself, did not steal, or illegally brand, a single calf. She bought them, as any other prostitute buys."

Kate and Jim never discussed the stolen cattle. The pair continued on as though the entire saga had never happened. Jim's loyalty to Kate, in spite of her infidelity, caused her to love him even more. She vowed to stand by him forever and do whatever was necessary to help him win his fight against the Wyoming Stock Grower's Association.

On July 20, 1889, a hot sun beat down on the ranch of cattle king Albert J. Bothwell. Members of the association had converged at his place for an emergency meeting. Albert convinced the members that in order to maintain control of the range, they needed to take immediate action against their most staunch opponents, Jim Averill and Kate Watson. "With those two out of the way, the other landowners won't dare stay on," Albert growled.

The association agreed to ride out to Jim Averill's place that afternoon and deliver one last ultimatum to the couple. They would give them a choice between leaving Sweetwater Valley while they still had their health or be forcibly ejected. The men knew Jim was a proud, fearless man who would choose the latter. Thus, Albert Bothwell threw a pair of ropes over his saddle and led the party on their way.

Meanwhile, Kate strutted proudly over the flower-covered hillside near her ranch, stopping occasionally to admire the beaded moccasins she had just bought from the Shoshone Indians encamped down by the river. Ranch hands John DeCorey and Gene Crowder were with her when the association members rode quickly past them. No words were exchanged.

When Kate, Crowder, and DeCorey reached her cabin, they found the association men waiting for them. Albert Bothwell leveled his gun at the three while one of the other men took down the gate around Kate's cattle and drove them out to the pasture.

"Get in the wagon, Kate," Albert demanded.

"Where we going?" Kate asked.

"Rawlins," he said with a wry smile.

Kate studied the faces of the angry men. "I'll need to change first. I can't go to Rawlins looking like this," she said.

"Get in the wagon now or I'll throw a rope around you and drag you the whole way!" Albert barked.

"What have you done with Jim?" Kate asked.

"Nothing . . . yet," Albert laughed.

Kate climbed into the wagon, and the group started out for Jim's place. They caught up with Jim as he was hitching up a team to drive to Casper for supplies and told him they had a warrant for his arrest. When he asked to see it, they patted their rifles and told him they were warrant enough. They made him get in the wagon with Kate and then drove off in the direction of Independence Rock.

Kate tried to move closer to Jim, but Albert Bothwell wouldn't allow it. The two exchanged a glance, and Jim forced a reassuring smile at Kate. The association members drove their horses up Spring Creek Canyon. Frank Buchanan, one of Jim's ranchhands, followed along behind the party, careful to keep a safe distance back and out of sight.

Spring Creek Canyon was dry, and the creek bed was clogged with high brush and gigantic boulders. Frank Buchanan got down from the saddle and, after tethering his horse, continued up the canyon on foot, hearing angry voices somewhere ahead of him. Using the boulders and brush for cover, he advanced until he caught sight of the lynch party and its victims. Lariats had been thrown over the limb of a scrub pine that projected out over the floor of the canyon from a limestone ledge. Frank opened fire on the mob, and they began shooting back. Seriously outnumbered, Frank decided to start out for Casper to get the sheriff.

"You're going to hang us, are you?" Kate snapped.

"Maybe we'll drown you," Albert Bothwell huffed.

Kate looked down at the shallow river below and chuckled. "Hell, there ain't enough water in there to give you hogbacks a bath," she quipped.

Albert gave the noose a hard tug. The bough above him bent under the strain. "How much you weigh, Cattle Kate?" he asked.

"You want to hold me on your lap and find out?" she snorted.
"Are you gents trying to make yourselves a rep? Are you respectable
cowmen ganging up and lynching poor little Kate?" she sneered. The
barb of contempt bit into the conscience of her audience. Frowns
deepened on tanned faces.

"I think the branch will do," Albert said.

A couple of association members led the wagon to the canyon
ledge, yanked Jim over to the rope, and slipped the noose around his
neck. "Don't worry, Kate. They aren't really going to hang us," Jim
assured her.

Albert threw a rope around Kate's neck and jerked it tight.
"You're wrong, Averill. You're both nothing but cattle thieves," he
snarled.

Kate cursed Albert and called the other men cowards. She
looked over at Jim and blinked away a tear. Jim half smiled as he
drank in her beauty one last time. He nodded to her as the association members pushed the two off the wagon. The pair didn't fall far
enough to break their necks; they strangled to death while the mob
watched. The angry ranchers left the scene, each going in a different
direction after vowing never to say a word about what they had done.

By the time Frank Buchanan returned to the site with the lawmen, Kate and Jim's lifeless bodies were swaying to and fro in a gentle breeze. Unbeknownst to the association, Kate's ranch hand, Gene
Crowder, had followed the men to the canyon and witnessed the
lynching. He came forward and told the sheriff what he had seen.
Warrants were issued, and news of the hangings spread quickly
throughout the West.

Newspaper readers were outraged that anyone would have
hanged a woman. The *Salt Lake Tribune* commented, "The men of
Wyoming will not be proud of the fact that a woman—albeit
unsexed and totally depraved—has been hanged within their

territory. That is the poorest use that a woman can be put to." The *Cheyenne Daily Leader* had a different take on the hangings.

> Let justice be done. All resorts to lynch law are deplorable in a country governed by laws, but when the law shows itself powerless and inactive, when justice is lame and halting, when there is failure to convict on down-right proofs, it is not in the nature of enterprising western men to sit idly by and have their cattle stolen from under their very noses.

Two days after Kate and Jim were hanged, their bodies were cut down. Kate's father arrived in Rawlins to claim his daughter's body, telling newspaper reporters that the cattlemen who accused his child of rustling were liars. "She never branded a hoof or threw a rope," he insisted.

Six men were eventually arrested, Albert Bothwell among them, but the legal process was a farce from the beginning. Rawlins authorities were "in the pockets" of the association, and the six defendants were permitted to sign one another's bail bonds. The witnesses against the guilty association members, including Frank Buchanan, began to disappear one by one. By the time the trial began, there was no one left to testify against the mob, and the defendants were discharged.

Jim's ranch house and store were torn down, and the lumber was carted away to be used a second time. Cattle Kate's small cabin was sold at auction for $14.19. The purchaser was Albert Bothwell. He had the building dragged to his ranch, where he used it for an icehouse.

A curious Rawlins citizen who visited the site where the couple was hanged retrieved the moccasins Kate had on when she died. They had fallen off her feet during the hanging. The moccasins are now on display at the Wyoming State Museum.

Kate and Jim were first laid to rest in shallow graves on Jim's land. A few years later their remains were moved to a cemetery in Casper.

Long after their deaths, the love and devotion the two had for each other continued to capture the hearts of cowhands and towns-people in the territory. Their romance was the inspiration for dime-store novels and campfire songs. In 1891 a poem written by an anonymous author about the lovers appeared in a Wyoming news-paper.

Before this mirage picture had I met her on the trail
Where she'd bought a herd of cattle
That was offered up for sale.
She trailed them to her ranch home
And before the brands were well
A band of whitecapped riders came
The rest is sad to tell.
They took her from her ranch home.
They also bound her mate.
Then they hanged big Jimmie Averill
And the fearless Cattle Kate.

Charles Goodnight

The Trail Driver and the Schoolmarm

The true woman is the foundation of all civilization.
—CHARLES GOODNIGHT

Charles Goodnight hoped to shield his new bride from the news that two men had been hanged from a telegraph pole near their honeymoon hotel room. He'd already dragged Molly hundreds of miles across the plains from Hickman, Kentucky, where they'd been married, to rip-roaring and wild Abilene, where no gentle lady like his wife was safe, and on across the western plains to Pueblo, Colorado, where the hotel proprietor's wife rushed in to tell the news Charles had hoped to keep secret.

It was hardly an auspicious introduction to the West, but Charlie was not one to sugarcoat the truth. He'd made a reputation as a straight shooter when he signed on with the Texas Rangers. He'd developed the Rock Canyon Ranch after years as a drover on the Goodnight-Loving Trail, which he'd forged with his partner, Oliver Loving. But he'd had little to do with women, and graceful excuses were as foreign to him as French cooking.

His new bride looked at him with her beautiful dark blue eyes, waiting for him to explain how in 1870 men could be strung up right in the center of town. Mary Ann "Molly" Dyer Goodnight was accustomed to a more refined way of life. Her father had been a respected lawyer who served in state government in Tennessee. Her family counted a governor among its members, and her five brothers had fought in the War Between the States.

Six-foot-tall, 225-pound Charlie Goodnight found himself stammering out the only positive thing he could think of about the situation, "Well, I don't think it hurt the telegraph pole." Instantly, he knew it was the wrong thing to say.

Molly stared at the large, capable man she thought she knew and wondered what she'd done by marrying him. Her comfortable life as a schoolteacher, surrounded by friends and family in Weatherford, Texas, seemed far in the past. She'd known Charlie Goodnight for six years. Having raised her five brothers following the death of their parents, she understood the ways of men. Faced, however, with the callous answer about the condition of the telegraph pole, Charlie, she feared, had been too long in the company of ruffians. She told him so and said she would not live in a place where people were hanged in the public streets.

Charlie agreed to everything she said, even saying he would take her back to Texas if she wished. But, he added, she must first rest from their long journey to Pueblo. Then he made sure she met all the "good ladies of Pueblo." It wasn't long before the plan to return to Texas was dropped, much to his relief. Everything he had worked for since his childhood was almost within reach.

Charles Goodnight started working at the age of eleven, when he hired out to neighbors near the Brazos River in Texas. As a teenager he worked as a drover, herding cattle and driving freight wagons. He also served as a scout and guide with Captain Jack Cureton's Texas Rangers. He and his partner, Oliver Loving, had established one of the first, and still heavily used, cattle trails in the West, and he'd made enough money to buy a ranch of his own. Now he was a married man with property in Colorado and grand ambitions for the future.

Mary Ann Dyer

For her part, after the initial shock, Molly settled comfortably into the ranching life near Pueblo despite the dissatisfaction of seeing her husband ride off on trail drives, taking skinny cattle with wickedly dangerous horns to market. As Charles developed the ranch and looked for ways to improve the breeding of his longhorns, Molly learned how to be a rancher's wife. She called the drovers who worked on the ranch her "boys," and it wasn't long before the term "cowboy" became commonly used.

Ranching was an uncertain business, and when bad times hit in 1873, Charles lost everything. He sent Molly to live with relatives in California and turned to the one thing he knew well: trail driving. He gathered 1,600 head of longhorns and moved them to New Mexico. From there he explored for the kind of grassland country he wanted as the location for a new ranch. By 1876 he'd explored the Palo Duro Canyon in the Texas Panhandle and decided it was an ideal place. He and his men built a dugout topped with cottonwood and cedar logs for shelter.

By that time Molly was ready to rejoin her husband. She wrote a letter advising him to either come back to civilization or meet her in Denver and escort her to the Panhandle. Charlie tried to explain that the trail was long and hard, a suitable house had not yet been built, and the nearest neighbor was 75 miles away, but Molly could not be put off any longer. She traveled to Denver, and Charles met her there.

While living in Pueblo, Charles had been introduced to a wealthy Englishman named John Adair, who wanted to get into the cattle business. Adair agreed to advance the money Charles needed to expand his new spread. They formed a partnership, and the grasslands ranch in Palo Duro Canyon became known as the JA Ranch. John Adair and his wife, along with Charles and Molly Goodnight, some of the "boys," and about one hundred Durham bulls set out for the Panhandle.

The cowboys could barely contain their amusement with the fact that they were off to start a ranch with a herd of bulls. But Charles knew the bulls could be used to build better cattle from the tough and rangy Texas longhorns he'd herded up the trail for years.

Molly, sitting on a wagon seat with heavy leather reins in her hands, watched the broad, high plains dip and swerve into deep canyons and narrow valleys near the Canadian River. Farther east lay the Palo Duro. She loved the wide-open space, but water was in short supply. They went two days without water before Charlie decided to scout ahead for a watering hole.

"We've got to reach water tonight, Molly," he declared before he left. Putting her in charge, he told her to aim for the point on the horizon where he would disappear from view. Meanwhile, he would find water and come back to guide the party to it.

Molly watched her husband disappear and marked the spot. The heat of the afternoon, the dust, and the bawling of the cattle combined with anxiety about the situation wore on her nerves, but she pressed the team forward. Suddenly one of the cowboys loped his horse urgently toward her wagon. Pointing into the distance, he said he'd seen Indians. Molly looked through her field glasses and saw what appeared to be a band in full headdress on the warpath.

She ordered the wagons into a rough circle and prepared to defend the outfit. She worried about her husband, the Adairs, the expensive bulls, and her boys, who remained vigilant against the threat. Eventually it appeared that the Indians had camped, but Molly decided to stay put.

Charles returned and was furious to find the wagons and stock had moved barely a mile from where he'd left them. He'd found water, but it was a long way off. Swearing in exasperation, he asked his wife what had stopped their progress. Indians, she cried, pointing to their campsite. Charles looked through the field glasses and swore again. It was nothing but a mirage, he said in disgust, just a clump of bear grass and heat waves.

Once again the wagons, drovers, and bulls set out, and eventually they reached water. The whole outfit rested for several days before starting toward the descent into the steep Palo Duro Canyon. When they reached the mesa overlooking the canyon, Charles was astonished to find the grasslands full of grazing buffalo, for by that time, most of the huge beasts had been exterminated.

Once again, Molly became uneasy. A storm was brewing, sections of the great buffalo herd were stampeding at the least provocation, and the noise the herd made was deafening. Part of the problem, her husband explained, was that the mating season was in full force, changing the usually placid nature of the beasts.

That night flashes of lightning lit up the wagons continuously and thunder boomed, making sleep impossible. Worried that the buffalo might stampede right over the wagons, Molly urged Charlie to do something. He got up and built a large fire to keep the herd away. It was a long time before she discovered that he did it only to make her feel better. The herd was miles away, down in the canyon.

A few days later, after the men had built a meandering, 4-mile-long road down into the canyon and had driven out the buffalo, the party descended to the river and built a two-room log cabin. The Adairs left later in 1877, and the Goodnights settled in for the winter.

The wind blew almost constantly in the canyon. Quanah Parker, son of a Comanche and a white captive, brought his band into the valley to hunt. Charles recognized that the Indians had a bleak future after following the buffalo herds for centuries. The herds were nearly gone, and the Indians were starving. Charles made a treaty with Quanah; the Goodnights would supply the Comanches with beef for a promise that they would leave the JA cattle alone.

Molly had no children of her own, but she was known for her mothering of cow and cowboy alike. She discovered an orphaned buffalo calf and convinced Charlie to raise it. From that calf began a buffalo herd that eventually became famous all over the world. At one point Charles crossbred beef cattle with buffalo, producing "cattalo."

Molly's nearest neighbors were 75 miles away, and for six months to a year she lived isolated from all but her husband and the cowboys. Three chickens delivered to her in a sack by a cowboy became her best friends. But Molly later said it was not a bad life, except for the outside dangers that worried her. Luckily, she had Charles, who was constantly watching out for her.

The risk Charles and John Adair took in starting a ranch in the rugged Texas Panhandle paid off. By 1882 the ranch cleared a profit of more than $500,000. Adair got most of the money, but Charlie, who took most of the risk and did all of the work, got a raise from $2,500 to $7,500 a year to manage the ranch. With shrewd purchases of land, the JA eventually contained more than 1.3 million acres.

Molly and Charles helped start Goodnight College, and a railroad town was named Goodnight in their honor. They were well known and respected all over the state of Texas. Charles presented Molly with a large clock inscribed to the woman he loved and admired:

IN HONOR OF

MRS. MARY DYER GOODNIGHT

PIONEER OF THE TEXAS PANHANDLE

FOR MANY MONTHS, IN 1876–1877, SHE SAW FEW MEN AND

NO WOMEN, HER NEAREST NEIGHBOR BEING SEVENTY-FIVE

MILES DISTANT AND THE NEAREST SETTLEMENT TWO

HUNDRED MILES. SHE MET ISOLATION AND HARDSHIPS

WITH A CHEERFUL HEART, AND DANGER WITH UNDAUNTED

COURAGE. WITH UNFAILING OPTIMISM, SHE TOOK LIFE'S

VARIED GIFTS, AND MADE HER HOME A HOUSE OF JOY.

When Molly died in 1921, Charles sat in grief-stricken silence in the church he and his wife had helped build in Goodnight. He disappeared before the funeral service was over, dry-eyed and alone, and went to sit beside the fire and listen to the lonesome ticking of Molly's clock.

Charlie seemed to lose heart after Molly's death. He became seriously ill, his magnificent physique gradually beginning to crumble. He hated doctors and refused to take medicine. Then a young nurse from Butte, Montana, with whom he had been corresponding because of their shared last name, arrived to nurse him back to health. On his ninety-first birthday, Charles married Corinne Goodnight. He died two years later, on December 12, 1929. In that final sleep he was laid to rest beside his beloved Molly in the Goodnight community cemetery.

The Sharpshooter and the Sure Shot

FRANK BUTLER AND ANNIE OAKLEY

What fools we mortals be! My admiration for Frank Butler's poodle led me into signing some sort of alliance papers with him that tied a knot so hard it lasted some fifty years.

—ANNIE OAKLEY, *THE STORY OF MY LIFE*, 1925

Frank Butler eased his lanky frame up a mossy bluff to Shooter's Hill. A small crowd had gathered on the wide porches of the shooting club, and the people applauded as Frank passed by. He tipped his green hat, with a jaunty feather sticking out of the band, to the cheering audience. He was an imposing figure with dark features and a tall build; he wore a belted hunting jacket and stylish trousers. Frank Butler was a professional sharpshooter—one of the best shots in the United States—and appeared in a traveling circus. He studied his surroundings as a chariot racer would study the track.

It was a beautiful Thanksgiving Day in 1875. An American flag flew from the flagpole on top of the clubhouse, red and yellow leaves drifted in from nearby maple trees, and a band played patriotic tunes as the last-minute details of the Oakley, Ohio, shooting contest were taken care of.

Jack Frost, hotelkeeper and organizer of the event, proudly marched over to Frank, grinning from ear to ear. "Ready for the match?" Jack asked.

"I am," Frank said, nodding.

"You'll be going up against one of my market hunters," Jack told Frank. "A fine shot. Every bird of theirs that comes through my place is shot clean through the head."

Frank nodded again and noticed that Jack was grinning like a cat that had swallowed a canary. "Something else I should know?" Frank inquired. Jack shook his head and tried to wipe the smile off his face. But his smile quickly broadened again when he saw Frank's opponent arrive on the scene.

She was fifteen years old and stood just under 5 feet tall. She had blue-gray eyes and chestnut hair. She wore a pink gingham dress and a sunbonnet to match. Jack introduced Annie Moses to Frank and announced that she was the shooter he'd be up against. Frank was surprised, but gracious. The referee called them to get ready, and the contestants took their positions.

The pair nearly matched each other shot for shot, rarely missing the clay pigeons that were catapulted into the sky. In the end Annie was the winner. A tremendous shout and torrent of hand-clapping rose from the crowds on the porch and on the grounds. Frank Butler turned to Annie, beaming, seemingly glad Annie had won.

"Great work, Missie," he said, shaking her hand.

"Thanks, Jimmy," she replied. In her confusion and excitement, Annie had gotten his name mixed up. From then on they were always Missie and Jimmy to each other.

Phoebe Ann "Annie" Moses was born to Jacob and Susan Moses on August 13, 1860, in Greenville, Ohio. Her parents were Quakers, and she was brought up in a quiet, religious manner. Jacob passed away when Annie was eleven, leaving the family of seven very little to sustain it. Susan went to work as a community nurse, but jobs were scarce and the pay small.

Annie Oakley

A year after her husband died, Susan remarried, but tragedy struck again when her second husband was killed in an accident, and she was a widow once more, with another baby to feed. Annie saw how her mother was struggling and wanted to help her family. She took a job as an assistant matron of an infirmary that housed the elderly, orphaned, and insane. Annie was good at her work and learned a great deal from her employer, including how to sew. Later, Annie took a position as a mother's helper, but the couple she worked for was not kind, and Annie eventually ran away. During her absence her mother married a third time. Back at home, Annie assumed many of the household chores, spending most of her free time with her only brother, John. John helped Annie use their father's gun to hunt rabbits for food. Soon Annie was an expert shot, supporting her entire family by selling game to storekeepers and hotel owners. It wasn't until Annie went to visit her sister in Oakley that she realized her skill with a gun was a talent that could open many doors.

Frank Butler was impressed with Annie's ability with a gun. Before he left Shooter's Hill he presented her with tickets to his show. Annie attended the program with her family. When Frank and his partners came out onstage, the audience erupted in applause. Frank put on quite a show—shooting objects out of the other marksmen's hands and splitting a playing card held edgewise toward him. Annie was captivated. For the finale Frank's white poodle, George, came forward and sat down on stage. An apple was placed on his head, and then Frank shot off the apple. Annie cheered wildly, and the whole audience joined her.

Backstage, Annie congratulated Frank on his "spectacular per-formance." Frank introduced her to his partners and to George, who came solemnly forward to Annie and presented a paw to be shaken. Frank was stunned. George generally did not like women, but he'd obviously taken a fancy to Annie. And so had Frank. Annie returned to Frank's show again and again. He and Annie became close friends, and on June 22, 1876, they were married.

Frank had a difficult time convincing Annie's mother to allow him to wed Annie. Susan did not think Frank was a suitable partner for her daughter. He wasn't a Quaker, was divorced with two children, in debt, and vaudeville was his career. Frank's persistence won her over. He promised Susan that he would do right by Annie and challenged her to put him to the test.

Frank was used to proving himself. He was an Irishman who had emigrated to the United States when he was just a boy. Unskilled but determined, he managed to support himself with a variety of jobs. First he delivered milk with a pony cart in New York City, next he was a stable boy, and later he became a fisherman. He knew he could make a good life for himself and Annie.

After they were married, Frank continued touring the country with his marksmen act, and Annie stayed behind with her mother. She went back to school to take up her education where she had left off as a little girl. Frank missed her terribly and would send gifts, letters, and poems frequently. On May 9, 1881, Frank sent her a poem that described his plans for their future.

> Some fine day I'll settle down
> And stop this roving life;
> With a cottage in the country
> I will claim my little wife.
> Then we will be happy and contented,
> No quarrels shall arise
> And I'll never leave my little girl
> With the rain drops in her eyes.

Many times Annie would visit Frank on the road. On one occasion Frank's partner became ill and couldn't go on. Frank persuaded Annie to perform in his place. When she walked out onstage, the crowd roared with delight.

Annie didn't miss a single shot, and the audience fell in love with her. By the end of the evening, Frank had made Annie his new partner. He changed her last name to Oakley, after the place where they had first met. Annie set about designing and making herself costumes that were more appropriate for their show. Their act was billed as "Butler and Oakley." Their poodles, George and Jack, appeared as a "specialty."

"Butler and Oakley" became the top shooting act in the country. They were offered a sizable amount to tour with the Sells Brothers Circus in 1884. At first Annie appeared only as an equestrienne, but Frank convinced the circus managers to allow his wife to add shooting from the back of her horse. The crowd loved it, and Annie became so popular people named her "The Queen of the Rifle."

Frank was proud of his wife but worried that she would tire of the vagabond lifestyle of an entertainer, which consisted of dusty trains, poor hotels, bad beds, tasteless food, and hours of practice just to keep the act fresh. Annie assured him that she was happy and considered traveling and performing around the country a marvelous adventure.

In her 1926 autobiography Annie expressed how much she loved their life on the road: "Any woman who does not thoroughly enjoy tramping across the country on a clear frosty morning with a good gun and a pair of dogs does not know how to enjoy life."

A performance in Texas in the later part of 1884 changed the direction of Frank and Annie's working relationship. Frank and Annie were doing their act before a group of rowdy cowboys. Frank

Annie Oakley and Frank Butler with one of their dogs

had struggled through his part of the routine, missing a few of his trademark trick shots. Annie's heart felt for her dear husband, but there was nothing she could do to help him.

A big, burly man in the crowd shouted out, "Sit down and let the little girl shoot." The man had a gun and looked as if he would use it if crossed. Annie hurried over to Frank and persuaded him to let her try the shot. She hit the target on her first try, and the crowd cheered.

Later, when the couple was alone, Frank took stock of the act and confessed to Annie that she was the better shot. "The people come to see you," he said. Annie tried to convince him that the crowds were there to see them both, but Frank knew that wasn't the case any longer. He knew the name Annie Oakley was becoming more and more famous with each show. Frank opted to step out of the limelight and become Annie's manager. Instead of shooting targets he would take care of her business matters. Annie reluctantly agreed, and from that time forward she did all the shooting.

Frank and Annie's tour with the Sells Brothers Circus ended in New Orleans in December of 1884. While there the pair visited the grounds of a competing show, Buffalo Bill's Wild West Show. Frank and Annie were impressed with the first-class care given to the animals in the show and the special attention paid to trick shooters and riders. Famed scout and guide Buffalo Bill Cody was equally impressed with the famous "Far West champion rifle shots." He hired the two, and Frank arranged to have Annie prominently featured in the show. Annie Oakley was the first white woman to travel with the Wild West outfit. Frank and Annie were well received by the other performers with the show and were always made to feel at home.

"So began our life with Buffalo Bill's Wild West," Annie later recalled. "The travel and early parades were hard, but we were happy. A crowned Queen was never treated with more reverence than I was by those whole-souled western boys."

Frank and Annie spent hours creating spellbinding bits for Annie's act. Frank originated many of her back-bending and mirror shots. He helped her perfect a routine during which she shot a hole in the center of an ace of spades that he held. Annie felt a sense of belonging in Buffalo Bill's show and reminded Frank of it often. "This is it!" Annie would say. "This is what we've been working toward. Here is where our act is most at home."

After several years with the Wild West Show, Annie and Frank suffered a devastating loss. George, their treasured poodle, died. George had been a part of their show and instrumental in bringing them together; he was like a member of the family.

"Frank and I buried him in a private lawn nearby," Annie remembered. "We put a pretty table cover under him and his beautiful satin and velvet cover with his name embroidered upon it over him. The Indian girls with the show made wreaths and chanted Indian hymns over him. Two of the cowboys lowered the little box to Georges last resting place."

Frank and Annie toured with Buffalo Bill's Wild West Show for seventeen years. They entertained world leaders, kings and queens, and kept company with celebrated Indian chiefs such as Sitting Bull. Annie had many admirers, and everywhere they traveled she was showered with flowers and gifts. Because Frank stayed in the background, many people did not know she was married. Annie received numerous love letters. One young man was so smitten that when he found out she was married, he fled to South Africa. Several years later he returned to the States, bringing with him as trophies horns from the game he had killed in Africa. He presented those trophies to Frank and Annie.

Frank Butler served his wife well as a manager. In between tours he would arrange newspaper and magazine interviews, matches, and exhibitions for Annie. He employed every proper method available to keep her name in the public eye, including putting her guns on display in various storefronts.

In 1890 a story broke that threatened to cripple Annie's career and undermine all the hard work Frank had done to promote her talent. "On Christmas Day in London I had just been helped to a platter of pheasant when a large tray of mail and telegrams was set before me," Annie remembered.

And some headlines running like this—"Annie Oakley dies of congestion of the lungs." Papers contained my pictures draped in flags. There were three telegrams from Colonel Cody, telling of his alarm at the report I was dead. Mister Butler, my husband, cabled back: "Annie just finished a full Christmas platter. No truth in report." Then the Colonel cabled: "Oh, I'm so glad Annie ain't dead. Ain't you?" The cause of the false report was the death of Alice Oatley, an American singer, and the names had been confused.

In 1899 Annie and Frank returned to the States and toured the country from New York to Nebraska. On July 25 Buffalo Bill and his "Congress of Rough Riders of the World" entertained in Annie's hometown of Greenville, Ohio. Frank and Annie received an enthusiastic reception. Annie finished her performance to a round of applause that rocked the stands. She was presented with a silver loving cup that was inscribed, TO MISS ANNIE OAKLEY, FROM OLD HOME FRIENDS OF GREENVILLE, OHIO. Annie motioned for Frank to join her in accepting the cup. She took his hand in hers and held it high overhead. The people in the stands threw their hats into the air with approval.

On October 28, 1901, Buffalo Bill's Wild West troupe boarded a three-unit train in Charlotte, North Carolina, for a trip to their last show of the season at Danville, Virginia. Several hours after the show train left the depot, it hit a freight train. There were no fatalities among the performers or crew, but 110 horses were killed outright or had to be shot.

Many people were injured, including Annie Oakley. When the trains collided, she was thrown out of her bunk and onto a trunk. Frank carried Annie out of the wreckage, and she was taken to a hospital.

She underwent surgery on her back and remained in the hospital for several months. At the time no one thought she would perform again. While Annie was mending, Frank took a job with a big cartridge factory and made plans for Annie apart from the Wild West Show. Toward the end of her recovery, Frank and Annie made the painful decision to leave Buffalo Bill's show. Frank's letter to Bill McCune, Colonel W. F. Cody's right-hand man, explained why: "It is like giving up a fortune to leave the dear old Wild West show; but a better position influenced us and we must go. Always your old friend, Frank."

The better offer was Annie's own show—a show in which she would star once she was well. Annie returned to work in January 1902, appearing in scheduled shooting matches and teaching children how to shoot. Frank and Annie toured the United States and abroad, and Annie dazzled audiences everywhere with her "sure shots."

Annie and Frank eventually grew tired of running their own show, and in 1911 they joined the Young Buffalo Bill Wild West Show and performed for large crowds across the West. At the end of that show's season, Frank and Annie bought a house in Maryland. When they weren't on the road, they rested in their elegant home while spending time with their dogs. Even though they were getting on in years, they never retired from performing and made many appearances at shooting expeditions and matches.

Frank and Annie eventually sold their home in Maryland and moved back to Ohio to be among friends and relatives. The two frequently visited family, helping them through illnesses and taking care of their children. In late October of 1926, Frank traveled to Detroit to visit Annie's niece. He said goodbye to his wife, not knowing it would be the last time he would see her.

On November 3, 1926, Annie Oakley died of pernicious anemia. She was sixty-six years old. Frank was so heartbroken when he got the news that he stopped eating. As a result he was too ill to attend the funeral. Annie's body was cremated, and her ashes were placed in a silver loving cup given to her by the people of France.

Frank Butler died seventeen days later. His body was brought back to Greenville, and services were held on Thanksgiving Day, fifty-one years after Frank and Annie had met.

Afterword

We have sought to illustrate some of the underpinnings of the familiar dramas of the Old West by identifying the real people who lived and loved in those times. The stories you have just read were put together using a variety of sources and are accurate to the best of our knowledge.

Trying to find out the truth about affairs of the heart conducted at a time when private conversation between an unmarried lady and a bachelor was practically prohibited is not an easy task. In some cases we have consulted multiple sources to determine the accuracy of different pieces of information. In other cases, such as the story of La Bonté and Mary Brand, the only source available is George Frederick Ruxton's book *Life in the Far West*, and he assures his publisher that the story is true; just the names were changed and the timing of events was slightly altered.

Research is made more difficult when personal papers are systematically destroyed, as were the letters and documents left by Marcus Daly. On the other hand, the huge amount of material in the Bidwell collection at the California State Library can feel like too much of a good thing. Sometimes one is left with more questions than answers, as in the case of beautiful Frances Allen, who seemed to attract men like a magnet, yet loved nothing more than the life of a prospector in the harsh conditions of the Arctic.

One of the interesting results of researching the love affairs of well-known characters, such as Doc Holliday, is uncovering letters and journals written by people who saw them in a different light than present-day historians. And although some questions inevitably remain unanswered, we hope these stories add another dimension to the understanding of our common heritage and capacity to love.

Bibliography

LaBonté and Mary Brand

Irving, Washington. *The Adventures of Captain Bonneville*. New York: G.P. Putnam, 1849.

Ruxton, George Frederick. "Life in the Far West." *Blackwood's Magazine*, 1848.

Wagner, W. F., ed. *Adventures of Zenas Leonard, Fur Trader and Trapper 1831–1836*. Cleveland, Ohio: The Burrows Brothers Company, 1904.

Jim Nugent and Isabella Bird

Barr, Pat. *A Curious Life for a Lady*. New York: Doubleday, 1970.

Bird, Isabella and Daniel J. Boorstin, ed. *A Lady's Life in the Rocky Mountains*. Norman, Okla.: University of Oklahoma Press, 1960.

Dunning, Harold Marion. *The Life of Rocky Mountain Jim*. Boulder, Colo.: Johnson Publishing Co.

Fort Collins (Colo.), *Express*, 8 and 15 May 1886.

Tinling, Marion. *Women into the Unknown: A Sourcebook on Women Explorers and Travelers*. Westport, Conn.: Greenwood Press, 1989.

Earnest Marks and Rosa May

Brown, Dee. *The Gentle Tamers: Women of the Old Wild West*. Lincoln, Nebr.: University of Nebraska Press, 1958.

Clegg, Charles and Lucius Bebee. *The American West*. New York: E.P. Dutton & Company, 1955.

Dary, David. *Seeking Pleasure in the Old West*. New York: Alfred Knopf, Inc, 1995.

The Ghost Town of Bodie. Bishop, Calif.: Chalfant Press, Inc., 1967.

Luchetti, Cathy and Carol Olwell. *Women of the West*. New York: Crown Trade Paperbacks, 1982.

Williams, George. *Rosa May: The Search For A Mining Camp Legend*. Carson City, Nev.: Tree By The River Publishing, 1979.

———. *The Red Light Ladies of Virginia City*, Nevada. Riverside, Calif.: Tree By The River Publishing, 1979.

John Rollin Ridge and Elizabeth Wilson

Browne, Juanita K. "*John Rollin Ridge*." *California Highway Patrolman*, #42 Edition, October 1978.

The Californians, November/December 1990 Edition.

Lardner, W.B. and M.J. Brock. *History of Placer and Nevada Counties*. Los Angeles: Historic Record Company, 1924.

McSwain, Elizabeth. "Member of Minority." *Arkansas Gazette*, 20 July 1941.

Parins, James W. *John Rollin Ridge; His Life and Works*. Lincoln, Nebr.: University of Nebraska, 1991.

Ridge, John R. *The Life & Adventures of Joaquin Murieta*. Oklahoma City: University of Oklahoma Press, 1854.

———. *Ridge Autobiography*. Fayetteville, Ark.: Fayetteville Historical Society, 1952.

Shields, Terrel. "Sarah B.N. Ridge." *Goingsnake Messenger*, Vol. XVII, Number One, 2000.

Wilkins, Thurman. *Cherokee Tragedy: The Story of the Ridge Family*. New York: MacMillan, 1970.

Ansel Easton and Adeline Mills

Harper's New Monthly Magazine. 1858. Courtesy of California Historical Library.

Johnson, William. *The Forty-Niners*. Chicago: Time-Life Books, 1979.

Kinder, Gary. *Ship of Gold*. New York: Vintage Books, 1998.

McCollough, David. *Path Between The Seas: The Creation of the Panama Canal 1870–1914*. New York: Simon & Schuster, 1999.

Seaman, Victor. *O Boys, I've Struck It Heavy! 1945*. Courtesy of Bancroft Library.

Story of an American Tragedy: Survivor's Accounts of the Sinking of the Steamship Central America. Columbus-America Discovery Group, Inc., 1988.

Thompson, Tommy. "America's Lost Treasure." *The Atlantic Monthly Press*, 1998.

Ware, Joseph. *The Emigrants' Guide to California*. St. Louis: J. Halsall Publishing, 1852.

John Bidwell and Annie Kennedy

Benjamin, Marcus. *John Bidwell, Pioneer, A Sketch of His Career*. Original publication National Tribune Co, Inc., Washington, D.C., 1907. Bidwell Mansion Association reprint.

Bidwell Diaries and Correspondence 1841–1900. Manuscript Collection, California State Library, Sacramento.

Daily Alta California. 3 August 1863; 18 and 20 July 1867; 5 and 7 May 1868.

Davis, Reda. *California Women, a Guide to Their Politics 1885–1911*. San Francisco: California Scene, 1967.

Hoopes, Chad L. *What Makes a Man: The Annie E. Kennedy and John Bidwell Letters 1866–1868*. Fresno, Calif.: Valley Publishers, 1973.

Howe, Edgar F. *Biographical Sketches; General John Bidwell*. Redlands, Calif.: The Facts, 1982.

Hunt, Rockwell. *John Bidwell, Prince of California Pioneers*. Caldwell, Idaho: Caxton Printers, 1942.

Rawlings, Linda, ed. *Dear General, The private letters of Annie E. Kennedy and John Bidwell, 1866–1868*. Sacramento: California Dept. of Parks and Recreation, 1993.

San Francisco Call, 5 December 1886.

San Francisco Chronicle, 10 March 1918.

Marcus Daly and Margaret Evans

Brothers, Beverly J. *Sketches of Walkerville*. Butte, Mont.: Ashton Printing & Engraving Co., 1973.

Emmons, David N. *The Butte Irish, Class and Ethnicity in an American Mining Town 1875–1925*. Chicago: University of Illinois Press, 1989.

Florin, Lambert. *Ghost Towns of the West*. Seattle: Superior Publishing, 1971.

Glasscock, C.B. *The War of the Copper Kings*. New York: Grosset & Dunlap, 1935.

Gocher, W.H. *Fasig's Tales of the Turf*. Hartford, Conn.: 1903.

Goodwin, C.C. "As I Remember Them—Marcus Daly." *Goodwin's Weekly* (Salt Lake City), 1913.

Liberty County Farmer. Chester, Mont. Undated clippings.

Powell, Ada. *The Days of the Bitterroot*. Privately published in Montana.

Progressive Men of Montana. Chicago: A.W. Bowen & Co., 1902.

Ravalli Republic (Hamilton, Mont.), August 1910.

Ravalli Republican (Hamilton, Mont.), 3 July 1987, August 1980, 19 January 1968.

Salt Lake City Tribune, 14 March, 28 April, and 16 May 1874.

Toole, Kenneth Ross. *Montana, An Uncommon Land*. Norman, Okla.: University of Oklahoma Press, 1959.

Utah Mining Gazette (Salt Lake City), April 1874.

Walter, Dave, ed. *Speaking Ill of the Dead: Jerks in Montana History*. Helena, Mont.: Falcon Publishing, 2000.

Doc Holliday and Kate Elder

Boyer, Glenn C. "On the Trail of Big Nosed Kate." *Real West*, March 1981.

Gray, John. *When All Roads Led to Tombstone*. Boise: Tamarack Books, 1998.

The Gunfighters. Chicago: Time-Life Books Inc., 1981.

Hickey, Michael M. *Street Fight in Tombstone*. Honolulu: Talei Publishers, 1991.

Jahns, Pat. *The Frontier World of Doc Holliday*. New York: Indian Head Books, 1957.

Kelly, Jack. "John Henry 'Doc' Holliday." *Georgia Press*, 1951.

Nash, Robert J. *Encyclopedia of Western Lawmen and Outlaws*. New York: Paragon House, 1989.

Robinson, Olivia. *She Did It Her Way*. New York: Putnam Press, 1946.

Jack Newman and Mollie Walsh

Dix, Milton. "West of Ours." *Portland (Ore.) News*, 1930.

Fitz, Frances Ella. *Lady Sourdough*. New York: MacMillan, 1941.

Foreman, Gene. *The Roundup; Wild West Stories*. Tacoma, Wash: Washington State Historical Society, 1931.

Hitchcock, Mary E. *Two Women in the Klondike, The Story of a Journey to the Gold Fields of Alaska*. New York: Putnam, 1899.

Holloway, Sam. "Mollie, Oh Mollie." *The Toronto Magazine*, Skagway Press, 1974.

Lynch, Frank. *The Shooting of Mollie Walsh*. Tacoma, Wash.: Washington State Historical Society, 1952.

Newman, Jack. "A Monument to 3,000 Horses." *Seattle Sunday Times*, 25 August 1929.

Williams, Scott D. *Murder, Madness, and Mystery*. Williams, Oreg.: Castle Peak Editions, 1991.

Tom Noyes and Belle Frances Allen

Daily Alaska Empire (Juneau), 31 October and 4 November 1952.

Letters of William Muncaster, Emma C. Patchen, Dr. William W. Graves, and Capt. W.H.K., Alaska Historical Library, Juneau.

Mining and Engineering World, February 1916.

New York Journal, September 1897.

Seattle Sunday Times, 14 June 1908.

Spokane Review, 22 September 1892.

The Spokesman (Spokane, Wash.), 15 June 1899.

Ward, Louetta. *Inventory of the Frances Noyes Muncaster Papers 1850–1952*. Juneau: Alaska Historical Society, 1985.

Zanjani, Sally. *A Mine of Her Own: Women Prospectors in the American West, 1850–1950*. Lincoln, Nebr.: University of Nebraska Press, 1997.

Jim Averill and Kate Watson

Anderson, Emory J. "Cattle Kate Did Not Deserve Name." Wyoming State Archives, 19 March 1978.

Carol, Todd. *Tragedy on the Sweetwater*. New York: Gutman, 1948.

Coates, Jim. "Cattle Kate's Murderers Were Never Brought to Trial." *Rawlins (Wyo.) Daily Times*, 22 January 1965.

"Cowboy Days Along the Sweetwater." *Wyoming State Journal*, 10 January 1932.

"Death of Cattle Kate." *Rivertown Ranger* (Wyo.), 6 August 1964.

"A Double Lynching." *Cheyenne Daily Leader*, 23 July 1889.

Koller, Joe. "Cattle Kate Only Woman Lynched in Old Wyoming." *Wyoming State Tribune*, 23 July 1940.

Nash, Robert J. *Encyclopedia of Western Lawmen & Outlaws*. New York: Paragon House, 1989.

Schmitt, Martin and Dee Brown. *The Settlers' West*. New York: Bonanza Books, 1955.

"The Sweetwater Lynching." *Rawlins* (Wyo.) *Daily Times*, 2 March 1976.

Wheelock, Billee. "Cattle Kate's Secret Found in Museum Here." *Casper* (Wyo.) *Tribune-Herald*, 20 March 1940.

Charles Goodnight and Mary Ann Dyer

Davison, E.J. "The Buffaloes of Goodnight Ranch." *Ladies Home Journal*. February 1901.

Denver Post, 22 July 1973.

Freeman, James. *Prose and Poetry of the Live Stock Industry of the United States*. Vol. 1. National Live Stock Historical Association, 1905.

Haley, James L. Texas, *From Frontier to Spindletop*. New York: St. Martin's Press, 1985.

Haley, J. Everetts. Charles Goodnight, *Cowman and Plainsman*. Norman, Okla.: University of Oklahoma Press, 1936.

"Handbook of Texas Online." www.ttsha.utexas.edu/handbook/online/ articles/view/GC/fgo11.html.

Kennedy, William. *Texas-Rise, Progress and Prospects of the Republic of Texas*. London: R. Hastings, 1841.

O'Neal, Bill. *Historic Ranches of the Old West*. Austin, Tex.: Eakin Press, 1997.

Stewart, Gail B. *Cowboys in the Old West*. San Diego: Lucent Books, 1995.

Frank Butler and Annie Oakley

Clegg, Charles and Lucius Beebe. *The American West*. New York: E.P. Dutton & Company, 1955.

Collier, Edmund. *The Story of Annie Oakley*. New York: Grosset & Dunlap, 1956.

Graves, Charles P. *Annie Oakley; The Shooting Star*. Broomall, Penn.: Chelsea House Publishers, 1956.

Gustafsson, Katie Anne. "Annie Oakley; Little Sure Shot." *Women's History Newsletter*, Cody, Wyo., 21 March 2000.

Interview with David Milles, Buffalo Bill Historical Center, 13 June 2000, Cody, Wyo.

Interview with Judy Logan, Garst Museum, 26 May 2000, Greenville, Ohio.

Oakley-Butler, Annie. *The Story of My Life*. Greenville, Ohio: Garst Museum, 1925.

Sayers, Isabelle S. *Annie Oakley and Buffalo Bill's Wild West*. Toronto: General Publishing Company, 1981.

Index

About the Authors

JoAnn Chartier

JoAnn Chartier is a broadcast journalist and talk show host living and working in California's Gold Country. Her writing has earned regional and national awards from professional associations.

Chris Enss

Chris Enss is an author and screenwriter who has had several scripts optioned and has won awards for her screenwriting, stage plays, and short subject films.

Chris Enss (left) and JoAnn Chartier

For more history of the Old West, the authors invite you to visit their Web site, www.gypsyfoot.com.